'If we're going to do this thing we really ought to know each other's names.' Stepping for ard, she put n Emily Ap

He t own work-rough ig her hand with g each other.

'Theo

'Okay, Theo, if you promise to pull out all the stops and let Lula hold her wedding here—including the use of your family chapel to hold the ceremony in if she wants to—we've got a deal.'

He gave her a discerning look. 'I'd have to square that with the vicar.'

'Then square it.'

He snorted in incredulity. 'She must be a very good friend.'

'She is.'

She'd swear that she glimpsed the glimmer of a smile in his eyes. So there *was* some life in there. He might come across as cold, and as hazardous as liquid nitrogen, but she could sense there was a lot going on under that tough surface. She'd bet her life on it.

The idea of breaking through the frigidity to uncover it made her whole body tingle with excitement.

'Okay, Theo, let's do it. Let's get romantic.'

Dear Reader

This is the second part of the first duet I've ever written—and I had so much fun with it! After she made a rather striking appearance in FIRED BY HER FLING, as Lula's best friend, I was desperate to give Emily her own happy-ever-after, and in BRIDESMAID WITH ATTITUDE I got my chance.

Emily is the epitome of an anti-heroine: she's bolshie, a little on the self-centred side, and very determined to get what she wants—no matter what it takes to get it. And I *love* her. She's had a very tough upbringing, but she hasn't let it beat her down, and even though it's made it hard for her to let people get emotionally close she lives her life to the max.

In order to force her out of her self-protective bubble she needs a hero with a determination to equal her own—and in Theo she finally meets her match.

These two challenge each other in ways they've never experienced before, and through dogged persistence—and some truly testing events—together they finally manage to overcome their worst fears and emerge on the other side as stronger, more confident and much happier people.

I hope you enjoy their journey as much as I did.

With best wishes

Christy x

BRIDESMAID WITH ATTITUDE

BY

CHRISTY McKELLEN

MILLS & BOON

Published in Great Britain 2014
by Mills & Boon, an imprint of Harlequin (UK) Limited,
Eton House, 18-24 Paradise Road, Richmond, Surrey, TW9 1SR

ISBN: 978-0-263-91160-2

Harlequin (UK) Limited's policy is to use papers that are natural, renewable and recyclable products and made from wood grown in sustainable forests. The logging and manufacturing processes conform to the legal environmental regulations of the country of origin.

Printed and bound in Spain
by Blackprint CPI, Barcelona

BK (Before Kids), **Christy McKellen** worked as a video and radio producer in London and Nottingham. After a decade of dealing with nappies, tantrums and endless questions from toddlers, she's come out the other side and moved into the wonderful world of literature. She now spends her time writing flirty, sexy romance with a kick (her dream job!).

Christy loves to hear from readers. You can contact her at christy@christymckellen.com, through her website, www.christymckellen.com, via Facebook, www.facebook.com/christymckellenauthor, or on Twitter, www.twitter.com/christymckellen

Other Modern Tempted™ titles by Christy McKellen:

FIRED BY HER FLING
LESSONS IN RULE-BREAKING
HOLIDAY WITH A STRANGER

This and other titles by Christy McKellen are also available in eBook format from www.millsandboon.co.uk

This one is for my fabulous courtesy cousins, Vanessa and Fiona, two of the strongest, smartest and kindest women I've ever had the pleasure to know.

CHAPTER ONE

EMILY APPLEGATE SWUNG her motorbike in through the open gates of the grand Buckinghamshire estate and screeched to a halt in the car park allocated to visitors, snatching the keys out of the ignition and dismounting in one smooth, practised movement.

Leaving her crash helmet swinging from the handlebars, she marched up the sweeping driveway towards the imposing Elizabethan mansion that sprawled like a hubristic monarch before her.

The heels of her biker boots dug into the golden gravel with a satisfying crunch as she made a beeline for the front entrance.

She was going to have someone's head—namely the stuck-up *Lord of the Manor* who'd had the gall to cancel her best friend's booking to use this grand house for her wedding reception only *one month* before the wedding.

Ignoring the glares of the two imperious-looking stone lions that guarded the door, she raised the heavy brass knocker and hammered it down hard three times, the tension in her fists matching the determined clench of her jaw.

You did not *do* that to a bride-to-be. Especially not someone as sweet-natured as her best friend Lula. The poor woman didn't need complications like this right before the most hotly anticipated event of her life.

She knew from numerous tipsy conversations with Lula over the years that her friend had been dreaming about her wedding day for ever. In fact the fantasy of *happy-ever-after* had been the thing that had helped keep her friend positive through an emotionally isolated youth with parents who didn't give two hoots about her.

Their miserable childhoods had actually been the common denominator they'd bonded over after meeting at university, and the fact that they understood and identified with each other's pain had kept them bound together ever since.

It was funny how they'd reacted to their loveless childhoods in totally different ways: Lula had been determined to marry well, and was convinced her life would be complete once she did, whereas *she* was determined *never* to rely on a man to make her happy.

The men she'd had relationships with over the years had only ever been interested in her as a good-time girl anyway; but that suited her fine. All she wanted were good times. There had already been enough bad to last her a lifetime.

And, anyway, she dealt with enough stress fighting to maintain her public profile as host of the popular TV show *Treasure Trail*. She certainly didn't need the added hassle of worrying about whether or not a guy was going to call her on top of that.

Not that she believed *every* man in the world was more trouble than he was worth. To give him his due, Emily knew that Lula's husband-to-be, Tristan, would have been here to sort this mess out himself if he hadn't been away in China on business. He was a good guy. One of the very few she'd met. She was glad to have the opportunity to step in on his behalf to help her friend with this crisis today. Lula wasn't exactly a big fan of confrontation—in fact, she knew the thought of coming here herself would have made her friend feel physically sick.

She missed their closeness now that Lu had Tristan to confide in. Lula was the only person in the world who really knew her—who really loved her for who she was—and she wanted her friend to know just how much that meant to her.

How much *she* meant to her.

She waited for a few more tense seconds before hammering on the door again, the noise making a dull reverberating echo somewhere deep in the heart of the building.

It sounded very empty in there.

A bit like its owner's head.

After another minute of frustrated knocking she became aware of a low rumbling noise coming from somewhere behind her. Turning to locate its source, she noticed an open door in one of the mews buildings that must have once been the stables for the estate.

Perhaps there was a groundskeeper in there who could point her in the direction of the troublesome toff of an owner, so she could let His Lordship know exactly what she thought of him for so casually ruining her friend's wedding plans.

As she approached the open doorway she could make out the figure of a man bent over some kind of industrial-looking machine as he worked with a large piece of sheet metal. She couldn't see his face clearly, because he was wearing Perspex goggles to protect his eyes and his jaw was covered in what must have been a week's worth of stubble, so her gaze roamed instead over the oil-stained white cotton T-shirt that stretched across his broad shoulders, then moved back up to his head of sandy brown hair that fell across his forehead in artful clumps, as if he'd deliberately styled it that way—although, based on the rest of his dishevelled appearance, she very much doubted that he had.

She watched with interest as he took a step to the left and seamlessly switched tools, the hand-held machine sending out a shower of sparks that filled the air with silvery-blue shooting stars.

There was no point in trying to grab his attention with all the pyrotechnics going on, so she settled in to ogle the rest of him instead, taking a moment to appreciate the strong contours of his frame: the dip of his waist leading to the lean line of his hips and the long, muscled legs encased in oil-stained, multi-pocketed combat shorts. She could see a spanner sticking out of one pocket, and what looked like a piece of torn sandpaper out of another.

Her gaze dropped further as she noticed a line of dripped grease on one of his robust-looking calves, and she fantasised for a second about what it might feel like to slide her fingertips over the oily toned muscles there.

She shivered in imagined anticipation.

There was something insanely hot about this man, looking all roughed up and dirty as he did, and a low, familiar throb began its beat between her legs.

Judging by her body's fiery reaction to him, it had clearly been far too long since she'd last had sex. After spending the last couple of months working flat-out filming her show, not allowing any distractions to tempt her, this guy appeared to have rekindled her voracious sexual appetite, and it was now back with a vengeance.

The sparks and noise stopped abruptly and he turned away from the machine to lob a heavy-looking clamp onto a bench to the side of him, where it bounced and settled with a loud *clunk-clank*.

Something was clearly bugging *him* today too, if the tension in those work-honed shoulders was anything to go by.

The hairs on the back of her neck lifted as she became aware that he'd finally noticed her standing there and had shoved his goggles to the top of his head so he could give her an impatient glare, one eyebrow raised in apparent annoyance at her unexpected appearance.

Looking at his face, now it was revealed in all its glory, she noted that he wasn't what she'd describe as classically handsome—he was a little too rugged, his features too irregular—but there was something darkly appealing about him. Something dangerous. Something devilish.

'Can I help you?'

His voice was low and husky, but it had the clip of good breeding about it. Perhaps the owner only employed people from the upper classes here, to make him feel more cocooned in his embarrassment of riches.

'I'm looking for the idiot who owns this place. Any idea where I can find him?' she said, flashing the guy a winning smile and walking further into the room. Just because she was mad at his boss it didn't mean she couldn't be friendly with him.

He pulled a rag from his back pocket and wiped his hands on it while he seemed to consider her question. 'What do you want with him?' He looked back up to meet her eyes, his gaze shrewd, as if he knew *exactly* what she'd like to do with *him*.

His eyes were the colour of the lichen that had used to grow on her family's Cornish beach house—a dense kind of greeny-grey with a hint of gold.

'From the tone of your voice, I'm guessing it's nothing good,' he added, shoving the rag back into his pocket, making the lean muscles in his arm twist and flex in the most appealing manner.

Shaking her head, she attempted to break the core-tightening hold he had over her and casually leant one hip against the workbench to steady herself. 'I'd rather save my wrath for the man in question. He has some serious grovelling to do.'

He raised one eyebrow. 'Intriguing. I'm sure he'll be delighted to facilitate your every whim.' The sarcasm in his voice was so heavy it could have sunk ships.

A loyal employee, then.

She shrugged, giving him a playful grin. 'He'll be fine as long as he gives me what I want. Otherwise I'm gonna have to tear him a new one.'

He raised both eyebrows this time. 'Sounds like I could be done for aiding and abetting a crime if I tell you what you want to know.'

'Don't worry—I won't implicate you.' She dipped her chin and gave him a wink. 'It'll be our secret.'

'How very generous of you,' he drawled, still not breaking a smile.

Man, this guy was seriously tough. And hot. And distracting her from her reason for being here.

'So where is *His Lordship*?'

Pulling the goggles from the top of his head, he tossed them onto the workbench next to her, not breaking eye contact for a second, his expression remaining impassive. 'Actually, you're supposed to address me for the first time as Lord Berkeley, and then as My Lord after that.'

She felt as though her legs had been taken out from under her. '*You?* As in, *you're* the Earl of Berkeley?'

What were the odds of Lord Snooty being so gorgeous?

He held out both hands in ironic surprise. 'What's the matter? Don't I look the part?'

She snorted. 'Not even close. Where's your paunch? Where's your receding hairline? You don't even have a ruddy nose or an inappropriate leer.'

'I'm sorry to disappoint you.'

'I never said anything about being disappointed.'

His brow pinched into a scowl and it suddenly occurred to her that she was flirting with the scoundrel who was messing with Lula's happiness when she should have been ripping him limb from limb.

'Although I *am* mad at you for ruining my best friend's wedding,' she added, perhaps a little too late to make much of an impact.

Advancing on him now, she raised an accusing finger and pointed it at the centre of his broad chest.

'What the hell do you think you're doing, cancelling her booking a month before the wedding? Do you have *any* idea how happy she was to secure this place for her reception, especially after all the hoops you made her jump through?'

He opened his mouth to speak, but she wasn't finished with him yet.

'Is this about money?' She ran her gaze over his dishevelled appearance. 'Has someone offered you more for that date? Because if that's the case you should be ashamed of yourself. You can't play with a woman's hopes and dreams like that; it's sheer cruelty!'

He sighed and leant back against the workbench, crossing his arms and making his muscles bulge under his tight-fitting T-shirt. 'She hasn't been gazumped.'

'Then why? *Why* would you do that to her?'

'Unforeseen circumstances.'

'What circumstances could be serious enough to ruin someone's wedding day over? She chose this place in good faith. You signed a contract.'

'Which gives me the option to cancel a month before the event. She'll get her money back.'

She took another step forward, going for *coolly menacing*, but he didn't move a millimetre. There wasn't even a flicker of a reaction on his face.

Her heart-rate picked up, chasing adrenaline though her body. This close to him she could make out the scent of grease and hard work that radiated from him, and it was doing something crazy to her libido.

What was it about this mixture of good breeding and rough façade that sent her into such a spiral of lust? Perhaps, having lived and mostly worked in London for so many years, she was too used to being surrounded by metrosexual men—men who would be horrified by the thought of being caught looking so unkempt. There was something oddly refreshing about this guy not appearing to give a fig about his appearance. He'd made no move to tidy himself up at all. He didn't care what she thought.

She kind of liked that.

Focus, Emily.

'All right, *Lord Berkeley*, it's not as simple as getting her money back and you know it. She's already sent out the invitations. People are coming from as far away as Australia. They've booked very expensive flights. And she's already confirmed food with the caterers, booked the cushion-fluffers and the petal-tweakers—the whole crazy shebang. She's been planning this day for a whole *year.* You're going to ruin the best day of her life.'

'She'll find somewhere else.'

Something flickered in his eyes and he looked almost

regretful for a second, until he drew the angry shutters back down on his expression again.

Emily huffed out a disbelieving laugh. 'She can't arrange another reception venue *now*; there's nowhere decent left to host that many people at such short notice.'

'That's not my problem.'

She clenched her fists in frustration, feeling her nails dig into her palms. Clearly he was going to be a tough nut to crack.

Okay, time to change tack and crank up the charisma she was so famous for.

Reaching out, she laid a palm against the rock-hard wall of his chest, right over where his heart would have been located if he'd had one, and brought out the big guns, giving him her most coquettish look. 'Is there some other way I can persuade you to change your mind? It would mean the world to her—and me—if you could find a way to let her have her reception here.'

She watched in surprise as he put his hand over hers, curled his fingers tightly around it and pulled it away from his chest, dropping it the second it was clear of his body. There was no gentle regret in the move; it was a pure and resolute rebuffal.

The rejection rankled. Men never normally turned her down when she was in full flirt mode. She understood the power she wielded with her face and her body and had utilised it well over the years.

Narrowing her eyes, she pulled back her shoulders and squared up to him. 'I don't get it—what's really going on here?'

He frowned. 'What do you mean?'

'There's more to this than sheer bloody-mindedness. It smells all wrong.'

His expression flashed with contempt. 'Because I won't submit to your womanly wiles?'

Hot indignation bubbled in her stomach, chased by a sting of mortification at being outed so bluntly. 'Because no one could be so evil as to mess with someone's wedding day without a really good reason.'

He snorted and pushed off from the bench, brushing past her to walk over to the other side of the room.

The brief contact made something pulse and tighten deep in her pelvis.

'It's out of my hands,' he said, his back to her, his upper torso tensing as he braced both arms against the window ledge and stared out through the glass. 'This house belongs to my mother, although she lives in Spain at the moment and is "allowing" me to live here until I inherit.'

His shoulders seemed to tense even more.

'She came over to England a few days ago, stuck her nose in here while I was away and discovered that I've been hiring out the place for wedding receptions without her consent.' He turned back to face her and she saw a flicker of embarrassment in his expression. 'She harangued my events manager until she gave up the details, then phoned around and cancelled all future engagements. I lost my phone in a cab while I was away, so I only found out about it when I got back last night.'

Emily stared at him in disbelief. 'Why would she *do* that?'

He sighed and rubbed a hand over his forehead, leaving streaks of grease over the ridges of his frown. 'She's punishing me for not bending to her will. She thinks I should be married by now and providing her with a clutch of adoring grandchildren.' His voice dripped with scorn.

'She's worried she's falling out of social step with the cronies she spends all her time lunching with.'

'And you're going to let her get away with it?'

His gaze snapped to hers and the indignation in his glare made a shiver run down her spine. 'You think I have any choice in the matter?'

If he thought he was going to get her to back down by being hostile he could think again. 'Why didn't you tell her about holding the wedding receptions here?' she asked, keeping her voice firm.

He sighed and swiped a hand through the air in irritation. 'Because I knew she'd put the kibosh on it. She considers the idea of making money out of the estate crass, and the notion of her son actually *working* for a living and "associating with riff-raff"—her words—horrifies her. I should be acting all *lordly* and extending the family line.'

'Didn't you see this coming, though? Surely you planned for something like this happening if you were keeping secrets from her? In my experience, secrets never stay buried for long.'

Although she'd somehow managed to keep *her* biggest secret buried all these years. She knew it was only a matter of time before it reared its troublesome head, though, and then she'd have some explaining to do.

Not that she should be worrying about herself right now. This was about Lula and what needed fixing.

He plucked the spanner out of the pocket of his combats and tossed it into the air, catching it, then tossing it again end to end as he spoke. 'She's been threatening to sell this place from under me for years if I don't fall into line, and I'm guessing it's all come to a head now because she's recently split up with her second husband. She's clearly bored with not having anyone to order around any more, so she's decided to spend her time making my life hell instead.'

Emily almost felt sorry for him as she noted the tension in his face. He looked tired—as if he hadn't slept well.

'Can't you reason with her?' she asked, more gently this time. 'Ask her at least to wait until after Lula's wedding?'

'I tried. No dice.'

'Is there anything *I* can do to persuade your mother to let Lula have her wedding here? If you think there is, just name it. I'll do anything.' She knew she was beginning to sound desperate, but there was no way she was just going to give in and walk away—not when she'd promised Lula she'd fix this. There was always a solution; sometimes you just had to think outside the box to find it.

He stopped tossing the spanner and fixed her with a seriously unnerving expression. 'Anything?' he asked, raising both eyebrows.

She took a breath, wondering what she was about to get herself into. 'Yes.'

'Then you're going to have to fall in love with me.'

Theo Berkeley watched in amusement as a range of expressions ran across the woman's face—from surprise, to disbelief, to confusion and back again.

She was quite something to look at: tall, with a curvy but well-toned body, and a head of long, blonde-tipped chocolate-brown curls. She also had the most striking eyes he'd ever seen. They looked golden in the meagre light trickling in through the workshop windows, and they glowed with the fiery determination that she'd repeatedly exhibited since walking in here.

She was for real—he could tell.

He'd met women like her before—one woman in particular from his past he'd rather *not* be reminded of had been very much like her—and it made him wary. So much so that when she'd made that move to touch him he'd instinctively snatched her hand away from his chest, as though it might burn him with the fever he felt flickering away at the edges of his memory.

This woman was dangerous, pure and simple, but he had an idea that he could use that to his advantage if he was careful. He needed someone like her—someone who wouldn't be afraid to stand up to his mother. Unlike the women he'd most recently dated. If he was going to make the crazy plan he'd been toying with for the last few minutes work, she needed to have the gumption and the initiative to be able to win over his fastidious mother.

Judging by the way she'd stood up to him this woman clearly had those qualities in abundance, and it seemed like a gift from the gods that she'd landed here in his workshop right when he needed her. It was fate.

Either that or he was being seriously punished for something.

She finally seemed to pull herself together and put out a hand to lean back on the workbench behind her, dipping her head and giving him an amused look. 'You're kidding, right?'

'Not kidding.'

'Why would you need me to fall in love with you?'

'I don't, really, but in order to get my mother off my back and be allowed to run this estate as I see fit I need to be able to produce a girlfriend whom she believes is a viable option for future nuptials and the furthering of the family line.'

She gave an exaggerated shudder at his crass analysis. 'Why do you need a *fake* girlfriend? Haven't you got the pick of a harem of women you can call on for just this purpose, *My Lord*?'

He raised a laconic eyebrow. 'Earls don't tend to have harems—you're confusing us with sheikhs.'

'And you don't have a real girlfriend to dangle under her nose?' she asked.

She was not rising to his sarcasm; which impressed him. Normally women would blush and stutter when he was in an irascible mood.

He gave a terse shake of his head. 'My life's complicated right now. I'm trying to build up this business and pay my overheads here. I don't need the added stress of a relationship.'

She narrowed her eyes, clearly seeing where this was going. 'But if you *did* have a girlfriend your mother would leave you alone and perhaps turn a blind eye to you holding wedding receptions here?'

'She could probably be persuaded to let a good friend of my *girlfriend* hold her reception here. That she could just about deal with, I'm sure. In fact she'd probably jump at the idea. It would give her a sense of power and control over you, which she could utilise in the future. You'd be indebted to her. She could use that to her advantage.'

She shook her head, her expression radiating disgust. 'How is she able to have so much power over *you*?'

'Because I've been disinherited and, according to my late father's will she legally owns this place and can sell it from under me at any time if the whim takes her. It's been her bargaining chip since my father died a few years ago. If I don't fall in line with her grand plans she'll take away my inheritance. I love this place. It's been my home since the day I was born and I'm not giving it up that easily. I want to grow my business from here and also raise the funds to be able to renovate the house sympathetically.'

'Seriously? That all sounds like something from the Dark Ages.'

He shrugged. 'She's been trying to manipulate me my whole life.'

'And you're not the type of guy to give in to manipulation,' she stated, giving him a wry smile.

He crossed his arms. 'I actively rebel against it.'

Her expression became serious. 'So, let me get this straight. You need to convince your mother that you're not the closed-off loner she thinks you are so she'll get off your back and let you live your life of happily single earldom in your mansion with only your tools for company?'

He fought hard against the smile that played at the corners of his mouth. 'Interesting choice of words, but in essence you're right on the money. So I need a girlfriend who will satisfy my mother but who won't expect anything to come from this. We'll pretend to be madly in love with each other while she's here visiting—which I'm hoping will only be for the next week or two—then, when she's safely under the illusion that I'm well on the way to marital bliss and has agreed to give me full control over how the place is run, we'll be able to call it quits. It'll be a purely business relationship.'

She widened her eyes. 'Wow. Cold. I'm guessing lines like that haven't had the desired effect on the women you've dated in the past?'

'Not exactly, no. For some reason the women I've been involved with recently seem to want hearts and flowers from me, and as I'm sure you've probably guessed by now, I'm not that kind of guy.'

She smiled. 'I have. Because I'm not that kind of guy either.'

He snorted. 'Sounds like we're meant for each other.'

She looked away from him, crossing her arms and frowning as if she was thinking things over.

'Surely this plan's only going to work in the short term? Won't she quickly move on to nagging you to set a wedding date?' she asked, fixing him with her mesmerising golden gaze again.

'Hopefully she'll be so busy trying to bag husband number three by then she'll leave me alone a while longer. The rest I'll have to play by ear in the future. I just need enough time right now to get my business off the ground and start making money. Then I'll be in a stronger negotiating position.'

The look she gave him was one of respectful awe. 'Okay, look, give me a few minutes to think over your madcap plan and I'll get right back to you.'

He raised an eyebrow. The mere fact that she hadn't already stormed away in disgust was encouraging. 'Sure. Take your time.'

'I'll be back.'

'I don't doubt it,' he said to her retreating figure.

Sighing, he rubbed his hand over his forehead, trying to relieve the achy tension there. The whole 'madcap plan', as she'd called it, was a long shot, but anything was worth a punt at this point.

After giving up a well-paid but mercenary job working for a blue-chip engineering firm in London, he needed to be left to his own devices here in order to build up his own fledgling business until it began to turn a decent profit.

The weddings had been a great source of revenue, but he wouldn't be able to go back to doing them until his mother was satisfied he was on his way to settling down.

What he'd neglected to mention was that the real reason his mother was keeping such a tight grip on his inheritance was because she was afraid he was going to slip back into the dark underbelly of the life he'd wallowed in a few years ago and fritter it all away on drink and fast women. He'd been a major source of embarrassment to her during those years, and she was determined not to allow him to put her through that again. Not that he intended to. Those crazy, hedonistic, sex-and-drugs-filled days were well and truly behind him now.

Turning back to the bandsaw, he ran another sheet of metal through it, finding a calming solace in the screech of the hard materials as they tore against each other.

Most unnervingly, the woman he'd just propositioned reminded him a little too keenly of the women he'd used to play with during that dark time, and he was aware he'd need to keep a firm grip on his impulses if he was going to stay on the straight and narrow with her around.

She had something about her that intrigued him. An iron will not dissimilar to his own.

Flicking off the machine, he put the two pieces of metal onto the workbench and started marking out where he needed to drill holes into them.

If she came back and said no, the only other option was actually to get married, so his mother would reinstate his inheritance—both money and estate—but he didn't want to do that for a number of reasons, the biggest of which was the fact that he'd never met anyone he thought he'd be capable of putting up with on a day-to-day basis. He liked his space, and he had a horrible feeling a wife would want to mess with his carefully constructed life plans.

It would be a cold day in hell, the day he bent to someone else's will again.

Emily paced around the well-manicured grounds of the manor house, her brain ticking over like a revved-up engine.

His idea wasn't *totally* insane. In fact she was quite excited by the thought of it—and not just because it meant spending more time with this inscrutable, scorching-hot man.

It wouldn't do her career any harm, being seen to be involved with an earl. Recently it seemed as though the press were growing bored with reporting on her whirlwind affairs with playboys and party animals—the type of men she associated with because they were easy company and didn't make any emotional demands on her—and she knew in her line of work it was imperative to keep her profile up in the press.

Recently the producers of her show had started to make worrying noises about her no longer fitting the tone of the show, and she'd heard through the production grapevine that they were considering offering her role to Daisy Dunlop—a recently retired athletics runner with a steady home life—once the show moved to the mainstream channel it was touted to be promoted to soon.

There was no way she was letting someone else get their hands on her baby. She'd worked long and hard to get where she was. The show *was* her and *she* was the show, and she could fit any box they needed her to in order to keep on hosting it.

It was just a case of proving to the producers that that was the case.

So she needed to clean up her act.

Perhaps serendipitously, Theo could be the answer to her problems. The press would jump on a story about her getting romantically involved with someone with his appeal and social standing, which could be the profile-boosting stunt she desperately needed if she was going to keep her career on the up-and-up.

Logistically it would work fine too. She had a few weeks off while they took a break in filming the show, so she had the time to hang out here with Theo. Despite his grumpy demeanour, she liked him—probably because he wasn't a push-over—and it wouldn't exactly be a hardship to hang out at his estate for a week, even if it *was* under the watchful gaze of his odious-sounding mother.

But most of all if faking her feelings for the Earl meant that Lu could have her dream wedding here then it would all be worth it.

Besides, it could be fun—and she was a big fan of fun.

Striding back into the workshop, she watched Theo for a moment or two, enjoying the spectacle of his lithe to-ing and fro-ing.

She cleared her throat to get his attention and he turned round to face her with a questioning expression.

'If we're going to do this thing we really ought to know each other's names.' Stepping forward, she put out a hand. 'Hi, I'm Emily Applegate.'

He took her hand, enveloping it in his own work-roughened one, and squeezed hard, coating her hand with grease so their fingers slipped against each other.

'Theo Berkeley.'

'Okay, Theo, if you promise to pull out all the stops and let Lula hold her wedding here—including the use of your family chapel for the ceremony if she wants it—we've got a deal.'

He gave her a discerning look. 'I'd have to square that with the vicar.'

'Then square it.'

He snorted in incredulity. 'She must be a very good friend.'

'She is.'

She'd swear that she'd glimpsed the glimmer of a smile in his eyes. So there *was* some life in there. He might come across as cold and as hazardous as liquid nitrogen, but she could sense there was a lot going on under that tough surface. She'd bet her life on it.

The idea of breaking through the frigidity to uncover it made her whole body tingle with excitement.

'Okay, Theo, let's do it. Let's get romantic.'

CHAPTER TWO

THEO FELT THE tension he'd been holding on to begin to dissolve as she said the words he'd been hoping to hear.

Still, there was one thing that needed to be established before they embarked on this little adventure together.

'Before we begin I want to make sure we've got this clear, Emily—I help you and you help me, then when it's over we walk away.'

'That works for me.'

'Are you sure? Because I'm not looking for a relationship right now.'

She let out a long breath through her nose, an expression of irritation taking over her face. 'Neither am I. Like I said, I don't do hearts and flowers either. It's not my style.'

The veracity of her statement came through loud and clear in the tone of her voice.

He nodded, feeling reassured that she meant what she said.

'Just out of interest, why is it up to you to sort out your friend's wedding venue? Shouldn't it be her husband-to-be turning up here, bargaining with me?'

She leant one hip against the wall and gave him a look from under her lashes. 'We thought you'd be more likely to want to sleep with *me*.'

He rolled his eyes at the trite joke.

'Seriously, though,' she said, grinning at his reaction, 'Tristan's away at the moment, and Lula has enough on her plate, so as chief bridesmaid I offered to come instead. Because she's the person I love most in the world. She's been my rock, and I want to do this for her because I know how devastated she'd be if her wedding plans went awry. She's had a pretty tough life and she deserves to be happy.'

The determination in Emily's face clinched it for him and the last bit of tension drained away.

'Okay, then we'd better get on with it,' he said, laying down the hacksaw he'd been clutching in his hand. 'We only have a short time to get to know a bit about each other. My mother's visiting friends today, but she'll be staying here later and it's probably better not to catch her on the hop. She doesn't like to be put on the back foot. I'll tell her about you first, and wait for her to insist on meeting you, then I'll suggest I invite you over tomorrow for Sunday lunch. We'll start small.'

'So we're not going to pretend I live with you here?'

'No. That would seem suspicious. She'd expect to have heard about you already if you'd moved in with me.'

'Still, you'd better show me around in case I need the loo or something when she's here and have no idea where to find it. That might look a little suspicious too.'

'Good idea.'

Walking over to a small sink in the corner of the workshop, he washed the grease off his hands before turning back and gesturing for her to step through the door. 'After you.'

They strolled side by side from the workshop to the front entrance of the house, with Emily craning her neck to look up at the impressive E-shaped building, with its gold-coloured stone, mullion windows and carved geometric frontage.

She let out a low, complimentary whistle. 'It's quite a pad you've got here, Theo.'

He experienced a surge of pride as he took the opportunity to experience the place through her eyes. After living here for the last couple of years, ever since his mother had moved out to go and live in Spain with her new husband, it was easy to look past the magnificence of the place, but he knew how special it was. He felt a deep and meaningful connection to the place, right down to his bones.

While he rummaged in his pockets for the keys she bent down and pretended to pet the stone lions that guarded the door. 'Hello again, my fine feline friends. Don't worry—I come here with the full benediction of your owner this time,' she purred at them.

He had a disquieting moment when he wondered whether he was crazy to put his faith in such an unknown quantity, and had to remind himself that he didn't exactly have a better option.

Opening the door, he ushered her inside and introduced her to the grand hallway, with its stone-flagged floor, dark wood panelling and arched stone doorways leading off to the downstairs rooms.

'This is where the tour begins.'

'Should I take my shoes off?' she asked, he suspected only half jokingly.

'No need. Let me show you the rooms down here first.'

He led her through to the drawing-room, then the morning room, pointing out the odd period feature, then the library—his favourite place after the workshop, which smelled like history—then finally the comfortable converted kitchen-diner.

'Very nice, Theo. I can see why Lula's so keen to have her reception here. All this dastardly scheming is definitely going to be worth it,' Emily said as she gazed around at the oak cupboards and bifolding doors leading out to a large tiled terrace which looked over the extensive gardens.

'Speaking of which—we ought to get on with it,' he said, aware that they had a lot to cover in a short amount of time.

She nodded. 'Yeah, if we're going to make this work we need to keep our stories simple.'

'Agreed.'

He gestured for her to follow him back out into the hallway.

'How about we met in London?' she said, walking to the bottom of the staircase and propping her elbow on the highly polished oak banister. 'Through a friend from university, perhaps?'

'That would work. I used to have a job in the City, so she'd buy that.'

'And we've been seeing each other on and off for a year?'

'Yes. The on and off thing is good. It adds credence to me not mentioning you already. We could have been "off" when I've seen or spoken to her in the past.'

'Okay. Good.'

He nodded towards the sweeping staircase. 'Come on upstairs with me while I change, and then I'll show you the bedrooms and bathrooms up there.'

'Lead on,' she said, and he felt her following close behind him as he mounted the stairs.

He stopped at the first door off the landing. 'This is me. I'll only be a minute.'

'Okay,' she said, surprising him by following him inside.

He turned and gave her a questioning frown.

'I should probably know what your room looks like,' she said with a pseudo-innocent smile. 'Just in case.'

He raised his eyebrows but decided not to kick her out. She had a point.

Emily stopped in the middle of the enormous wood-panelled bedroom and watched Theo disappear through a door on the far side, which she guessed must lead to his en-suite bathroom and dressing room.

'Take a look around if you want. I removed all the dead bodies yesterday, so I don't have anything to hide.'

His voice sounded muffled, as if he had his head in a wardrobe. Then she heard the sound of the shower being turned on.

She smiled and did as he suggested, walking around the room and peeking into a couple of his drawers, finding only some paperbacks and a handful of pens in them.

His bed was enormous and comfortable-looking, and made up with what looked like Egyptian cotton sheets and a large duck down duvet. She walked over and picked up one of his pillows, holding it to her nose and breathing in the manly scent of him. It had some kind of exotic undertone, like lemongrass or lime—something fresh and clean like that.

Something delicious.

Her whole body flooded with hot longing as she thought about getting close enough to him to smell it on his body.

The shower was turned off.

Tossing the pillow back onto the bed, she crept over to the door of the en-suite bathroom to see whether she could catch an illicit peek at him as he dried and changed, her nerves humming with anticipation.

'Find anything of interest?' he asked loudly, and she took a couple of quick steps away in case he came out and caught her spying on him.

'Not a thing—you've been very thorough,' she called from the safety of the middle of the room.

There was a pause, then a bang like a door closing, and then he spoke again. 'You know, I think our biggest obstacle in making this thing work is that my mother's a snob, and that means any girlfriend I have needs to come from a family good enough to meet with her approval.'

His voice was clearer now, as if he was standing right on the other side of the door.

She'd just opened her mouth to reply when he strode back in, wearing a pair of antique wash jeans and a slim-fitting black shirt, left open at the neck, exposing the deep hollow of his throat.

'Er…we…er…don't need to lie about that,' she managed to utter through a mouth that appeared to have stopped working properly.

He'd been gorgeous in his work clothes but he was absolutely glorious in urban chic, with his damp hair all mussed and falling into his eyes.

He raised a questioning eyebrow and she realised she was staring at him with her mouth hanging open.

'I mean, I actually *do* come from a good family and I was sent to all the "right" schools.' She made the quotes sign in the air with her fingers. 'Plus, my father's the CEO of a very well respected accounting firm in the City.'

He nodded. 'Good, that will make a difference.'

She looked down and kicked at a bit of fluff on the carpet with her toe. 'Of course I haven't spoken to him in ages—or my brother, for that matter. He's been living in Australia for the last six years, so we're not exactly on great terms. And I guess I need to tell you that my mother's dead.'

She no longer felt the throb of brutal torment whenever she said those words. They just rolled off her tongue, unencumbered.

It worried her some days how numbed she felt to it now.

'I'm sorry.'

She looked back up to meet his concerned gaze and gave a twitch of her nose and a shrug of her shoulder to intimate that she was unbothered by it. 'Don't be. I'm not some delicate little flower that needs protecting. I can look after myself. Been doing it for years.'

He held her gaze, his brow furrowed as if he was trying to work her out. She stared back at him, determined not to be the one to look away first.

Finally he gave her a sharp nod. 'Do you want a drink?' he asked abruptly.

Clearly she'd passed some kind of test. Either that or she'd freaked him out by getting a little *too* personal and he was backing the hell off. 'I could murder a vodka and tonic,' she joked, flashing him a cheeky grin.

He raised an eyebrow. 'I was thinking coffee. Very strong coffee.'

'Very strong coffee would work too,' she said, giving another indifferent shrug.

He snorted gently. 'Okay, I'll show you the rest of upstairs, then we'll go back to the kitchen.' He walked out of the room, leaving her to follow behind.

She caught him up as he went into the next door along the corridor. 'Guest room,' he said, waving a hand around the room.

'Nice,' she said, nodding sagely. She wasn't joking either—the whole place was beautifully done out.

'So, what's your big secret, then, Theo? Hmm…? Everyone has one? Let me guess.' She folded her arms, tipped her head to one side and gave him a contemplative stare. 'A brood of illegitimate children just poised to crawl out of the woodwork? Or perhaps a mad wife stashed away in the attic?'

'*Unlikely* to the first guess and *not yet* to the second, but I'm sure it's only a matter of time.'

'Because you're bound to drive any woman you get involved with round the bend?'

'Something like that.'

His gaze raked her face for a moment before the corner of his mouth twitched upwards. It was the closest thing she'd seen to a smile since they'd met and a sense of satisfaction warmed her blood.

He must have been uncomfortable with the change in atmosphere, though, because he brought down the frown again, then abruptly turned and walked out of the room, leaving her to hurry after him.

Back out on the landing, he gestured down the corridor, pointing out the other guest bedrooms and bathrooms, then strode off back down the stairs—presumably to make the promised coffee.

She caught up with him as he reached the bottom step and followed him into the kitchen, where he proceeded to set up the coffee-maker.

Turning to look at her once it was gurgling away, he narrowed his eyes, as if deciding how to put his next statement. 'Not meaning to be insensitive, but we'd better not go into detail about your lack of family harmony in case my mother thinks you're after me for my money,' he said finally.

She snorted and crossed her arms. 'I don't need your money. Not with the job I have.'

'What job is that?' he asked, leaning back against the counter.

'You really don't recognise me? Emily Applegate from *Treasure Trail*? It's one of the most popular shows on TV at the minute.'

At least it was on the second-rate channel it ran on—but, to be fair, it was soon to be promoted to the big league. There was no need to mention the small hiccup of the threat of being dropped from the show to him, though. It would only complicate matters, and they'd agreed to keep their stories simple.

He scowled. 'Never heard of it. I don't watch television.'

'You *don't watch television*?' She took an exaggerated step back and threw out her hands in mock shock.

He grunted in response and turned away to pour them both a mug of coffee. 'I have better things to do with my time,' he said over his shoulder.

'Like tinkering with your tools?'

He turned back and handed her a mug, which she took gratefully, inhaling the wonderful aroma deep into her lungs.

'Like making equipment for people with mobility issues to help give them some freedom,' he said.

That brought her up short. 'Impressive.'

He shrugged the compliment off as if it meant nothing and gestured for them both to sit down at the large oak table in the middle of the room.

'So what led you to the business of making mobility aids?' she asked, once they were settled.

'I had an older brother who had severe mobility issues. I used to invent things to help him get around and carry out what we think of as easy day-to-day tasks so he didn't feel so trapped and frustrated. I found I was good at it, and I enjoyed it, so I went on to study engineering at university.'

'And your mother was okay with that?' she asked, blowing across the top of her drink to cool it down before taking a sip.

'Not really. She wanted me to go into politics. But I studied at Cambridge, and appeared to be rubbing shoulders with the right people, so she let it slide.'

'Where's your brother now?'

'He died when I was twenty. He had a lot of health issues so it was always on the cards.'

'Sorry to hear that.'

He shrugged and looked down at his coffee. 'Life can be cruel.'

'But you're actively doing something to make a difference to people who've caught a bad break—that's admirable.'

He took a long sip of his drink, his brow furrowed as if he was thinking about what she'd said. 'I'd like to do more but it's a long game, building up a business in this tough financial environment. I do a lot of work pro bono, because the people who need help the most are usually the ones that can't afford it. They often need things custom-made to suit the ergonomics of their house. Everyone's needs are different. Occupational therapists do a wonderful job, but there's only so much they can achieve with their limited funding.'

'Is that why you've been hiring this place out for weddings?'

'Yeah—in an attempt to keep up with the running costs of this place, and my living expenses, until the business starts making money. And also because I like to see the place full of life. It seems perverse for me to be rattling around in it on my own all the time.'

'If you're so worried about it being too big and expensive for you why don't you move out to somewhere smaller?' she asked, taking another gulp of coffee, enjoying the smoky taste of it on her tongue.

He looked at her as though she was mad. 'Because this is my ancestral home. It's been in the Berkeley family for four hundred years. My mother's not interested in living here any more, and if I wasn't here she'd probably sell it to the highest bidder. I'm not about to let some money-focused developer get their grubby hands on it and turn it into apartments or a golfing hotel.' He pulled his face into a grimace.

'Not a big fan of golfing?'

'No.'

'Balls too small?' She couldn't stop a wide grin from spreading across her face.

He gave her a warning frown. 'You're going to have to watch your mouth around my mother—she's pretty uptight.'

'Don't sweat it. I will,' she said, draining the last drop of her drink and managing to spill a bit on her top.

'And you're going to have to scrub up your appearance in order to impress her,' he said, indicating her torn jeans, biker boots and the wide-necked T-shirt hanging off one shoulder, flashing her bra strap.

Emily waved a breezy hand in the air. 'Not a problem. Don't worry, I'll have her wrapped around my little finger in half a day, max.'

'You're very sure of yourself.'

'Why, yes I am.'

An expression of approval flashed across his face. 'I like it.'

She leant forward, narrowing her eyes and forcing her lips into a soft pout. 'I know you do.'

His approval was quickly replaced with a frown. 'I'm not going to sleep with you, Emily.'

She let her mouth fall open in exaggerated shock, hoping like mad that he hadn't caught on to the mortified disappointment that had flashed through her at his abrupt rejection.

'Why ever not? Surely that's one of the perks of our arrangement?'

He leant back in his chair and crossed his arms. 'I don't make it a habit to sleep with women I've just met.'

She gave him a scrutinising look, brazening it out despite the unfamiliar turmoil she was struggling to deal with. Surely she hadn't lost her touch when it came to charming men? It had never deserted her before. Sex was the one area of her life where she felt she had absolute control, and she wasn't about to let him chip into it.

'You mean with women you don't *trust*?'

His expression didn't flicker, but she could tell he was holding something in. It was there in the rigidity of his jaw.

'What happened to you?' she asked.

'Nothing I want to talk to you about.' He got up and dumped his coffee mug in the sink.

She stood up too and followed him over to the sink, putting her mug next to his and standing a little closer than was absolutely necessary, just to see if she could get another rise out of him. She was having some trouble holding her nerve in the face of his steely resistance, but there was no way she was backing down from it.

Looking up into his face, she gave him a wry smile. 'Women, huh? We're nothing but a bunch of harpies and hangers-on.'

The corner of his mouth twitched—she was sure of it.

Score.

'What are you afraid of?' she asked, putting her hand on his arm and feeling his tricep tense.

'I'm not *afraid* of anything. I just prefer to get to know someone before I have sex with them. It's a matter of principle.'

She gave a mock teasing pout. 'Damn your principles.'

He fixed her with a long, hard stare that made her quiver inside.

'I'm sure you'll be able to control yourself. And, while we're discussing it, I want you to agree not to get involved with anyone else while we're doing this thing.'

'What?'

'If you're on TV there's a chance the papers might report on any hook-ups you have. I don't want my mother to hear about them. It would ruin what we're trying to do here.'

'So I have to promise to be celibate till this thing is over?'

'Yes.'

'And you seriously won't help me out?'

The impulse to push him into submission was too strong to ignore. She needed to win this now, for the sake of her pride. She ran her fingers gently up and down his arm, feeling him tense even more under her touch.

'You're going to leave me in a state of sexual frustration? So cruel!'

He grabbed her arm, wrapping his fingers around her wrist and pushing it against her own body, imposing a barrier between them. 'I'm sure you can find some other way to satisfy your carnal urges. There are tools for every job. Be creative.'

'It's not the same.'

'You'll survive.'

She huffed out a sigh, hoping he couldn't feel the tremble in her hand. 'Okay, but you have to promise to be celibate too…until this thing is over.'

'That won't be a problem.'

She shook her head in disbelief. 'Are you made of stone or something?'

'It *has* been suggested,' he said, releasing her arm and walking back to the table to push the chairs back under it.

'Look, if you're worried this is actually some elaborate plot to trap you into marriage and steal all your money, then don't be. I have plenty of my own money. I don't need to steal someone else's.'

'It never crossed my mind,' he said, his back to her.

She couldn't tell if he was being serious. His tone was so dry it almost cracked the air.

He turned back, his expression closed. 'We've probably got enough information to go on for now,' he said, 'and I have things I need to deal with before my mother comes back.' He pointed a finger at her in a commanding manner, as if she was a naughty puppy. 'Wait here.'

She watched him stride out of the room, wondering what he was going to fetch. A horse whip, perhaps? Or a pair of shackles? The mere thought of it only intensified the low hum of erotic tension that had plagued her all afternoon.

How could he be immune to the heat between them?

Perhaps she'd pushed him too hard, too fast? Normally it wouldn't bother her if she made a man uncomfortable with her brazenness, but she didn't want to jeopardise this thing with Theo.

Truth be told, she was flabbergasted by his assertion that he wouldn't sleep with her. No one had ever turned her down before, and the challenge of getting him to change his mind had now embedded itself firmly in her mind.

She really wasn't looking for anything serious, so why

the heck shouldn't they have some fun together? There was clearly a spark of attraction between them, even if he was refusing to acknowledge it.

It wasn't as if she was under any illusions about where she fitted in the grand theatre of life. She saw herself as the ruthless ex-lover that sweet, wholesome women saved their damaged alpha conquests from. In fact it amused her to think of herself as the facilitator of other people's Happy-Ever-Afters.

According to the gutter press she had loose morals, but she didn't cheat or mess around with men already in relationships—that was where she drew the line. She didn't *need* undying love from a man; she needed hot sex, excitement and new experiences. The men she dated usually served that requirement, but unfortunately they tended to be self-absorbed and rather vacuous.

Theo was a whole other proposition. Smart, philanthropic *and* attractive. It was a heady mixture. One she was keen to have a lick of.

He returned a moment later, pen and paper in hand.

'Write your phone number down on here and I'll call you later to confirm the details about tomorrow,' he said, dropping them onto the table.

She dipped into a low curtsey. 'Yes, M'Lord.'

He flashed her a disparaging look, clearly not in the mood for any more teasing. 'Let yourself out.'

Swivelling on the spot, he marched away, his feet making a heavy slapping sound on the flagstone floor.

'You've been a great audience,' she called after him, making sure sarcasm dripped from every syllable.

When she got home to London, the first thing Emily did was call Lula to tell her that she'd ninety-nine per cent sorted out the wedding reception venue problem.

'Just give me a couple more days and I'll have it all wrapped up and reconfirmed. Don't worry, it'll happen—I'll make sure of it.'

'How the heck did you swing it, Em?' Lula asked, her husky DJ's voice light with relief.

'I used my feminine wiles,' she replied, experiencing a surge of relief to hear her friend sounding so happy again.

'Please tell me you didn't sleep with him.' Lula's tone was jokey, but there was just a hint of expectancy in it.

'Of course not. I just made a very good case. He *is* rather gorgeous, though. In fact he's asked me out on a date. I'm going over for Sunday lunch tomorrow.'

'Jeeze, Em, you're a fast worker.'

'What can I say? Zee guys, zay *luurve* me!'

'So they should. You are a total goddess.'

'Why, thank you, my darling. Anyway, I'd better scoot—got to get my beauty sleep if I'm going to impress His Lordship tomorrow.'

'Okay—night, babe.'

'Nighty-night.'

Emily had just ended the call when another number flashed up on the screen.

'Hello?'

'Emily, it's Theo.'

Her chest did a strange squeezy thing at the sound of his voice. 'Hi. So we're on?'

'I told my mother about you. I said I'd been keeping you quiet because I wanted to be sure about committing to you before introducing you to her.'

'And?'

'As predicted, she wants to meet you. I think she's a little suspicious about how I've suddenly produced you out of thin air and wants to make sure she's not being taken for a ride.'

'Smart woman.'

'That she is.'

'So should I come for lunch?'

'Yes. Get here for midday tomorrow and be ready to turn on the charm.'

She pinched her nose to make her voice sound nasal. 'Wilco, My Lord. Coming through, loud and clear.'

'Emily?'

'Yes, my darling?'

'You're starting to worry me.'

She laughed. 'Chill out, Your Earlness, it's going to be fine.'

CHAPTER THREE

THEO WAS FINISHING up a job in his workshop before lunch the following day when Emily strolled in, looking for all the world like a demure, rich debutante in a strait-laced knee-length skirt, smart high-heeled shoes and a soft pink blouse which was buttoned up nearly to her neck. She'd tamed her wild curls into a sleek-looking knot on top of her head and her make-up was subtle and sparing.

She'd tied her personality down tight.

He felt oddly disconcerted by it.

Frustratingly, he'd not stopped thinking about her since he'd left her in his kitchen the day before, forcing himself to walk away from the bone-rattling sexual tension between them before he did something stupid like acting on it.

'You're early,' he said, glancing at his watch to confirm it was only eleven-thirty.

She shrugged. 'I didn't want to be late and get off on the wrong foot with your mother.' She picked up a pair of his goggles from the workbench next to her. 'I guessed you might be in here, playing with your tools,' she said, holding the goggles up to her eyes and making a ridiculous-looking face at him.

He rolled his eyes and walked over to grab them from her, dumping them back onto the workbench.

He liked it that she was comfortable enough with her looks to know she could get away with making herself look stupid and not lose any of her appeal, but he didn't want to encourage her in case she did it in front of his mother. She liked ladies to be just that—ladies—and she wouldn't see the funny side of any larking about.

The goggles had left a smudge of dirt on Emily's nose, where they'd pressed against her skin, and without thinking he swiped his thumb gently over it, wiping it away.

She stared up at him with those striking eyes of hers and for a second he couldn't move. It was as if she'd caught him in a tractor beam.

'Where's your mother?' she asked, her voice low and seductive.

They were standing so close he felt her breath on his skin.

A tug of longing pulled hard, deep inside him. 'In the house.'

She smelt amazing—like a spring garden in full bloom.

'We should probably get into character now, then, so we're comfortable walking in there together,' she said, and without warning she leaned up and forward on her toes, aiming her mouth to connect with his.

This time he reacted quickly, moving his head away from hers and putting a hand on her shoulder to keep her at a distance.

'What are you doing, Emily?'

'I'm greeting you in the manner of a devoted lover.'

'I don't kiss women I don't care about.' He refrained from adding *any more*.

Her brow pinched in jokey frustration. 'You and your crazy rules.'

He couldn't stop a snort of mirth from escaping. 'You're very forward.'

She gave a nonchalant shrug. 'I like sex and I'm not afraid to ask for what I want.'

'That much I already know.'

She let out a low sigh and took a step backwards, breaking the connection of his hand on her shoulder. 'I don't get it. I'm single, you're single—what's the problem?'

'I told you: this is a business relationship. I'm not looking for it to develop into anything more.'

'You know, usually the only time men act as if they don't like me is when they want me but think they're not allowed to have me.'

He folded his arms in front of his chest. 'You really believe I think I'm not *allowed* to have you?'

'Perhaps. There has to be some deep-seated angst simmering away under that tough outer shell of yours.'

'Maybe I don't find you attractive.'

She narrowed her eyes and gave him a discerning smile. 'Maybe.'

'Why do you want to sleep with me so badly?'

'Because you won't let me.' Her grin was wide and authentic. 'I'm just messing with you, Theo,' she said, slapping him gently on the arm.

He huffed out a laugh and tried to ignore the way his body had hardened in response to her teasing. No way was he letting her get into his head, and he definitely wasn't interested in allowing her to flatter her way into his bed. He'd been burned like that before.

'Although I haven't had sex for *months*,' she continued, giving him that coy look she'd tried on him when they'd first met. 'I've been too busy at work to have any kind of fun outside it.'

The heat in his body seemed to increase tenfold. He pushed away the feeling. 'Speaking of life outside, I checked you out online. You have quite a presence in the gutter press.'

She shrugged and glanced away. 'I used to. I haven't done anything outrageous recently, so they've grown a little bored with me.'

'Cleaning up your image?'

Her gaze met his again, square in the eyes. 'I just haven't found anyone interesting enough to play with.'

The underlying suggestion of *until now* hung heavily in the air between them.

He shrugged it off.

'It might be a sticking point for my mother if she checks up on you and sees the sort of exposure you've had in the past.'

'Surely the fact you've tamed the wild child in me will be a plus point? It's one of those fantasies, isn't it? A strong alpha male showing a fallen woman that she's worth more than she thinks she is? Usually by being spectacular in bed,' she said pointedly, waggling an eyebrow at him.

He snorted and shook his head. 'What kind of books have you been reading?'

'Actually, I don't read as much as I used to. I never seem to have the time, what with my job being so all-consuming. But I have a *vivid* imagination.'

His heart-rate spiked as he entertained the sort of things she might be imagining right at that moment. Turning away from her, he grabbed his keys from a hook on the wall, painfully aware that he needed to get out of there before this little sparring match moved on a step—in the wrong direction.

'Then why don't you wait here and use it while I have a quick shower next door?'

Her brow pinched into a confused frown. 'You're going to your neighbour's house for a shower?'

'I meant the building next to this one. It's a small guesthouse in the grounds.'

'Like a granny annex?'

'If you like.'

'I bet it's bigger than my house in London.'

'Probably.'

It was her turn to roll her eyes this time.

'I won't be long. Then we can go into the house together as if you've just arrived and I bumped into you on the way back over.'

'Good plan, Stan.'

He walked out of the door, shaking his head.

In the guesthouse, he took a quick shower and shaved off the stubble his mother had been so vociferously horrified about since she'd arrived. He hated the thought of having to toady to her, but he didn't exactly have a choice. He'd do just about anything if it meant she'd go back to Spain and leave him alone.

He wondered how his mother would to react to Emily. At this point it could go either way.

Hopefully if she *did* like her she'd fall for her quickly, because the thought of having to control himself around Emily for very much longer made him edgy.

He understood what kind of a person she was; he'd got her measure the first time they'd met. She was the type who, at parties, when someone arrived wearing a hat, took only a short time to charm it off their head and end up wearing it herself. The kind of woman who knew how to utilise a prop. The kind of woman who got what she wanted, one way or another. It was a real skill, he would happily acknowledge that, but the *look at me* attitude made him uncomfortable. Perhaps because *he* was now the type of man you would always find in the kitchen at parties, avoiding the determined advances of women desperate to get into his good graces and reap all the benefits an earl had at his disposal.

His natural inclination was to circle the edge of the action, watching and commenting from the sidelines, choosing his moment to shine. Emily was clearly the type who threw herself into the fray and rode the lulls and peaks like the accomplished social surfer that she was. She was also the type of person everyone hoped would turn up, because she made fun things happen.

With or without a hat.

He could imagine she was a queen at bringing the buzz, and that when you were in her favour you felt like the luckiest and most fascinating man alive, but when she grew bored being relegated to the shade of her presence would feel very cold indeed. He could do without getting involved with someone like that again.

He was already cold enough.

When he got back to the workshop a few minutes later he found her sitting on a stool at the back of the room, reading something on her smartphone.

She glanced up when he walked over to her and did a double take.

'Whoa!'

He raised both eyebrows in question, wondering what the exclamation was for. She was staring intently at him again. It had freaked him out a little last time, but he was growing used to it—and her—now.

'You shaved,' she said, sounding surprised.

'I have been known to behave like a human being sometimes.'

'It suits you. Your face. It's a good face.'

He gave her a baffled smile. 'I'm pleased to hear it.'

Despite his reluctance to let her get to him, he found her overt appreciation of him uplifting.

'I mean, stubble looks great on you, but you have a strong, manly jaw, so you look good without it too. Very good, in fact.'

He shifted uncomfortably, not sure what to do with the compliment. 'Okay, well, if you've finished assessing my face perhaps we should get on with this thing.'

She flashed him a grin. 'I'm finished.'

'Are you ready to meet my mother?'

She jumped off the stool and straightened her skirt. 'As I'll ever be.'

'Okay, then, let's do it.'

As they strode together towards the house Emily couldn't help but take another sneaky look at Theo out of the corner of her eye. He looked so different without his stubble—younger and brighter somehow, as if the devil had left him.

Not that it made him any less attractive.

Once he'd inserted his key into the lock and pushed the heavy door open she slid her hand into his and held on tightly so he couldn't shake her off.

'We're a devoted couple, completely in love, *remember*?' she muttered when he scowled at her in annoyance.

He had to be the least tactile person she'd ever met—something she felt compelled to work on with him. No wonder his mother thought he'd never settle down with a woman if he treated them all as coldly as he did her.

They both looked up as a figure appeared at the top of the stairs and began to make her way down towards them.

'What do I call your mum?' Emily hissed at him. They'd forgotten to discuss it, she realised, and she didn't want to get a simple detail like that wrong right at the beginning. It could sow a seed of discontent, which would be hard to uproot.

'Start with Lady Berkeley and let her correct you if she wants to. But don't hold your breath that she will,' he murmured back, his breath tickling her ear and making her stomach swoop with nerves just before his mother reached the bottom of the stairs and made her stately way towards them, a look of cool interest on her face.

Emily smiled warmly. 'Lady Berkeley, it's wonderful to meet you at last. Theo's told me so much about you.' She held out her hand to the woman, who looked at it with slightly affronted disdain before offering her own.

'Has he?' she stated dispassionately, barely giving Emily's hand a touch before dropping it.

'All good things, I assure you.'

'I doubt that.'

Ouch. The woman was as cold as ice.

Emily felt Theo shift beside her and forced her mouth into a wider smile. 'I'm Emily,' she said, to cover the tense silence that now hung between them all.

'Yes, I know. Theo told me all about *you*.'

'All good?' She gave the woman a hopeful look.

The Dowager Countess's mouth moved up a millimetre at each corner.

Oh, goody, another tough nut to crack. Not that she'd expected anything different from Theo's mother—he'd given her enough warning about her.

'What he didn't tell me was how you've managed to get him to forgo his determined *bachelor* ways,' Lady Berkeley said finally, pronouncing the word as if it horrified her.

'I charmed you—didn't I, darling?' Emily cooed, turning to Theo and giving his hand a squeeze, appreciating the comforting strength of his solid presence next to her in the face of his mother's unfriendliness.

'I'm not sure "charmed" is the word I'd use,' he replied, squeezing her hand back a little harder than was absolutely necessary, making her blood pulse through her body in the most disconcerting way.

'Says the man who refers to getting married as "future nuptials and the furthering of the family line",' Emily countered, flashing him a grin and digging her nails into the back of his hand in response to his jibe.

He made his mouth smile, but it didn't reach his eyes.

'So, the two of you have talked about getting married?' the Dowager asked, surprise clear in her voice.

'We're both open to the idea—aren't we, darling?' Emily said, feeling Theo stiffen beside her.

'Yes,' he said, shooting her a warning glare that thankfully his mother didn't pick up on.

'Well, at least you've got him to talk about the possibility of marriage. No other woman ever has,' Lady Berkeley said curtly. 'Shall we go through to the drawing-room for pre-lunch drinks? The staff finally seem to be doing their jobs properly now I've had a word with them.'

Without waiting for a reply his mother swept out of the hallway and into the drawing-room, leaving them to follow in her wake.

'Why on earth did you let her think an engagement was imminent?' Theo whispered, pulling Emily to a stop before the doorway and dropping her hand.

'I didn't feel I had much choice. She needed more convincing. The most important thing is to get her to take me seriously first—then, once I've got her on side, I'll use the full force of my charm on her.'

Theo threw up his hands in frustration. 'Heaven help

us all if it comes to a showdown between you and my mother.'

'What? You don't think I could take her?' Emily pretended to square up to him.

'Oh, I'm sure you'd put up a good fight, but my mother's a tiger.'

'Then I shall have to sharpen my claws,' she said with a smile. 'Look, just let me lead the conversation and keep out of it as much as possible. Don't rise to anything she says. Can you do that?'

'Yes,' he said through gritted teeth.

She nodded and turned her back on him, walking off through the doorway that the Dowager Countess had disappeared through, trying not to let his delicious citrusy scent distract her from the task at hand.

Lady Berkeley had already rung for the housekeeper to come and serve them drinks and had made herself comfortable on one of the sofas when they joined her.

Following her lead, Emily asked for a gin and tonic. Theo declined a drink, leaning back on the sofa opposite his mother with his arm resting along the back. His body language was dominant, but detached. Emily perched next to him and pinched her knees together primly, smoothing down her skirt and making sure she wasn't showing too much leg. She was so acutely aware of Theo, *right there* next to her, that she worried for a second that it might affect her concentration.

Buck up, Em.

When she glanced up Lady Berkeley was giving her another coolly assessing look.

'You know, you seem very familiar,' the woman said, narrowing her eyes.

'That's because I'm on TV. I'm the host of *Treasure Trail*—'

The Countess flapped a dismissive hand in the air. 'No, that's not it. I don't watch trash on television. I have better things to do with my time.'

Emily couldn't help but turn to Theo and murmur, 'You really are your mother's son.'

He scowled back at her.

'What did you say your surname was?' The Countess asked.

A slow trickle of discomfort ran down Emily's spine. There was something in the woman's face that made her nervous—as if she was running through a database in her mind of all the undesirables she'd logged there. 'I didn't.'

Theo's mother sighed, as if she was fed up with dealing with a recalcitrant child. 'Are you hiding your roots from me deliberately?'

Emily bristled. 'No, of course not.'

Although, actually, she kind of was.

'My surname is Applegate.'

His mother stared at her for a few beats, her eyes still narrowed. 'It doesn't ring a bell, but your mannerisms are so familiar. I just can't place you. I've got a sneaking suspicion it might have been someone from my schooldays. Where did your mother go to school?'

Hot fear gripped her. 'She went to a school in France. Beauville or something like that, I think.' She plucked the name wildly out of the air. 'But *I* was educated at a boarding-school here in England. There are some wonderful schools here, aren't there?' she said, determined to take control of the conversation.

The Countess gave a curt nod of agreement.

'Sadly, my mother passed away a few years ago,' Emily added, hoping to appeal to the woman's nurturing side and divert the conversation away from the specifics of her family's background.

'Hmm…' Lady Berkeley was still looking at her as if trying to figure something out.

There was a chance that she *had* known her mother, and if she worked out why—taking into consideration how judgemental the woman appeared to be—they could be in trouble.

Thankfully, Theo's housekeeper came back in then, to announce that lunch was ready, and they all got up and trooped through to the grand dining-room.

The long table in the centre of the room was only set for three people, and Theo first pulled out a chair for his mother at the head of it so she could sit down, then one for Emily.

'Thank you, darling,' Emily said, giving him a wink and leaning forward to give him a friendly peck on the lips, like any loving girlfriend would—which he avoided by turning his face at the last second so she got his cheek instead.

She got another lungful of his fresh citrusy scent as she pressed her mouth against his freshly shaved skin and her whole body flared with lust. Through her haze of need she felt him put both hands on her upper arms and guide her down into her chair, then he walked round to his own seat opposite her.

His determination not to let her kiss him only made her want to do it more. She was going to make sure she got a kiss from him by the end of today or she'd explode with frustration.

The Countess rose again with a frustrated sigh, muttering something about not having the correct cutlery, and strode over to the wall to ring the bell for the housekeeper, giving Emily the opportunity to lean across the table and mutter, 'Your mother is going to think something's not right if you won't kiss me back.'

He fixed her with a hard stare. 'I'm not kissing you, Emily, so stop trying to get me to.'

'I'm telling you, she's going to get suspicious. You need to get past your boorish pride and into the role of loving boyfriend if we're going to pull this off.'

The Countess returned a moment later, and Theo stood until she'd settled herself back into her chair with a loud sigh of dissatisfaction.

Theo set about pouring water for them all, and the poor harangued housekeeper appeared a minute later and replaced the cutlery with the set the Countess wanted, then hurried off to fetch the first course.

Emily noticed with surprise that Theo made sure to thank his housekeeper thoroughly after she'd served them, and even managed to swap a sympathetic eye-roll with her without his mother seeing.

Something tightened in her chest as she watched the exchange and she realised it was because she wanted him to act that way with her too. Ever since they'd walked into the house it had felt as if he'd put up a wall of ice between them.

Slipping off one of her shoes, Emily stretched out her leg under the table and slid her foot up his shin to his knee. He glanced up at her, his pupils large and dark with warning. She let her foot rest on his knee for a moment, feeling him reverberate with tension, and gave him a wide smile, daring him to do something about it.

He moved back in his chair, just out of touching distance of her foot, and raised a faintly mocking eyebrow at her.

The rekindled connection made her grin with satisfaction.

But as much fun as it was, torturing Theo, she was acutely aware that she needed to keep her eye on the prize here. Her main priority was to win Theo's mother over so she could gain permission to hold Lula's wedding reception in the house, so as soon as everyone had started eating she launched her charm offensive.

'You must be so proud to have raised such an honourable man as Theo, Lady Berkeley. I think it's wonderful that the livelihood he's chosen makes such a difference to other people's lives.'

The Countess arched a perfectly plucked eyebrow. 'My son has made some *interesting* choices. I'm sure if it had been left up to him he would have given all our family's money away by now. He doesn't seem to be able to recognise a sob story for what it is, or turn down a damsel in distress.' She gave Emily a pointed look.

Out of the corner of her eye she noticed Theo stiffen, as if he was steeling himself not to retaliate.

'Some people would count those as admirable qualities,' Emily replied, straightening her leg again and rubbing her foot against his calf in sympathy, only to feel a sting of hurt when he shifted his position away from her touch. Not that she should be taking it so personally. It wasn't surprising he was on edge. His mother was something else, having digs at him like this in front of his *girlfriend*.

'Hmm, as long as you know when and where to draw the line,' his mother stated coldly, seemingly oblivious to the game of defensive footsie under the table.

Despite his rejection of her support, Emily still had the strongest urge to stick up for him. 'Theo tells me he used to make some wonderful inventions for your older son. I'm sorry, by the way, for your loss.'

It was the first time she'd seen a flicker of genuine emotion on the woman's face.

The Countess dropped her gaze to the table. 'Yes,

Hugo died young. That's why it's so important for Theo to start thinking seriously about having children. He's the only male heir left in the Berkeley family.'

'I can understand why you'd be so upset at the thought of the family line ending. And for this place to be sold to someone outside the Berkeley lineage.' She swept her hand to encompass the whole room. 'It's a beautiful house. In fact…' She took a deep breath. 'My best friend is getting married soon and she's looking for a place to hold her wedding reception. This house would make a wonderful wedding venue.'

The Countess gave Emily her characteristic narrow-eyed look. 'Theo knows how I feel about hiring this house out for *events*.' She spat the word out as if she found it distasteful.

A pulse beat hard in Emily's temple as she fought the urge to give the woman a good old-fashioned telling-off and instead concentrated her energy on formulating her next tactical move. 'Yes, of course. I totally understand that. But surely you wouldn't mind us holding a reception here for a good friend of ours? It would be a very strict guest list, of course—only a few very special, very *select* people.'

Lady Berkeley gave her a hard stare, before finally saying, 'I'll think about it.'

Emily clapped her hands together, attempting to imply utter delight. 'That would be wonderful of you.' So it was going to have to be a softly, softly approach, then. Her heart sank. She'd hoped to be able to win the woman over faster than this, but clearly that wasn't going to happen.

An overwhelming sense of frustration threatened to drag her down, but she beat it back. So what if it was going to take a bit more effort to clinch the deal? She was game for it.

Time to redouble her efforts.

As they continued through the meal Emily finally found some common ground with Theo's mother by chatting about going to the Cheltenham races each year, and they were able to discuss horses that they'd backed and even hats they'd worn. By the end of lunch she almost had the woman eating out of her hand. At least, if not actually that, she'd come an awfully long way since that frosty greeting at the door.

She gauged that it probably wouldn't be a good move to push the wedding venue issue again today though, in case she sounded too desperate. This whole situation called for some very delicate handling.

'Well, I really ought to get back to London,' she announced finally, placing her linen napkin on the table beside her empty dessert bowl.

'You must come back and have supper with us on Thursday,' the Countess said, not bothering to clear it with Theo, who had opened his mouth at the suggestion, then closed it again as if he'd remembered he was meant to be sitting this one out.

Clearly he'd been having real trouble keeping his opinions to himself and his control under wraps, judging by the tension on his face.

'That would be lovely, My Lady,' Emily said, producing what she felt must be a spectacularly sycophantic smile.

'Oh, call me Francesca,' Theo's mother invited, her voice much warmer after their lunchtime natter.

Emily had to restrain herself from punching the air in triumph.

Francesca walked with Emily and Theo to the hallway, still talking about a horse she'd owned a few years ago.

'It was lovely to meet you, Francesca,' Emily said once they'd reached the front door.

'Likewise.' Francesca gave a regal nod. 'I'll let Theo see you out. I'm going for a short rest,' she said to him, sweeping off towards the stairs without a backward glance.

Theo couldn't quite believe what he'd seen unfold before his very eyes.

Emily had somehow managed to charm his mother, and even though she hadn't yet been successful in getting her to agree to allow her friend to hold her wedding at the house he didn't think it would take too much more pushing before she did.

She was incredible.

She was also the most frustrating woman he'd ever met in his life. All her teasing, on top of his mother's vicious jibes, had left his head and body buzzing with adrenaline.

His jaw was actually aching from biting his tongue so hard.

Bored with all the horse talk at dinner, he'd found himself trying not to let his wilful imagination run away with the notion of how good it would feel to strip Emily of those prim clothes and give her what she seemed so keen on getting from him. The repeated contact of her wandering foot had kept him constantly aroused and on edge, until he'd felt as if he was buzzing with the strain of holding himself together. All he'd wanted to do was grab hold of her and drag her out of the room.

And then what?

That he didn't want to think about.

'I'll walk you to your car,' he said as they watched his mother mount the stairs on her way up for her afternoon nap.

'Okay.'

She looked a little disappointed at being sent away, but he'd reached his limit of being around her.

At least of *controlling* himself around her.

They walked out of the door and down the driveway to where she'd parked her cherry-red Fiat 500. He guessed she'd come in her car this time, because she couldn't get her leg over her motorbike in that tight skirt.

Down boy.

'So,' Emily said finally, shooting him a grin once they were far enough away from the house not to be overheard. 'How did I do?'

'Fine. I think she likes you.'

She gave a startled laugh. 'You *think*?'

He shrugged nonchalantly, not willing to concede how amazing Emily had been. It would only make her more cocky, and he didn't think he could deal with any more of her lip right now. Not when he was feeling so damn edgy already.

'No thanks to you, I might add,' she said, narrowing her eyes. 'She never would have guessed you even find me attractive if we hadn't told her.'

Frowning, Theo looked straight ahead, determined not to let Emily get to him. 'I'm not a demonstrative person. She would have been suspicious if I'd been all over you.'

'Hmm…'

She picked up his hand and ran a fingertip across his palm, causing prickles of pure pleasure to bump along his nerve-endings. 'It wouldn't kill you to touch me once in a while, though.' She looked up at him through her lashes. 'Did I mention that I like a man who's good with his hands?'

'You don't give up, do you?'

She grinned. 'What can I say? I'm a very tactile person. I need to be touched. It energises me.'

'Yeah, you're a real live wire.'

'Don't I get a reward for winning your mother over so convincingly?'

His pulse picked up at the teasing suggestion in her voice. 'You think you deserve a *reward* after torturing me all afternoon like that?'

She gave him a wide, lazy grin. 'Call it a punishment if you want. Whatever floats your boat.'

Her eyes held a challenge he was struggling to refuse.

He shouldn't do it.

He mustn't let her get to him.

She kept looking at him with that taunting expression of hers, as if she knew exactly what he wanted to do to her but didn't believe he had the balls to go through with it.

Adrenaline surged through his veins, making his heart race and his breathing quicken.

He lost it.

Grabbing her wrist, he dragged her into a small copse of trees next to where her car was parked and swung her round so that her back was pressed against the trunk of a large oak tree. Pinning her wrists against the rough bark, he held her there, staring into those wide, mesmerising eyes of hers.

For a moment he froze, wondering what the hell he was doing, but then she moved her head forward, as if to try and kiss him, and his animal instincts took over again.

He was the one in control here.

He pulled back, spinning her round so she now faced the tree, then stood behind her and made her press her hands flat against the trunk.

'Don't move,' he instructed into her ear, and felt her

shiver with anticipation as he slid his hands down the length of her arms.

Reaching forward, he found the front of her blouse and pulled it roughly open, tearing the delicate material away from the buttons that held it together. Her bra was made from a smooth silky material and had an underwire in it. He pulled it roughly up and over her breasts, exposing them to his roaming hands.

Emily dragged in a ragged breath as he swept his palms over her nipples, feeling them harden under his touch, before cupping her breasts and lifting the heavy weight of them up and against her body.

She groaned low and deep in her throat, causing his already aroused body to spring fully into action.

He wasn't going to give in to it, though. It wasn't worth the trouble that came with it. He knew that from experience.

Releasing his hold on her breasts, he slid his hands down over her firm stomach, then skimmed her hips and moved his hands lower over her thighs, to find the hem of her skirt, yanking it up so it gathered around her waist.

'Yes…*yesss,*' she hissed through her teeth, her pleasure at being handled like this clear in her voice.

He tapped her ankles with his foot, commanding her to widen her stance, which she did without a murmur of protest.

He was reluctant to give her what she wanted right away, feeling a devilish need to give her a taste of her own medicine, so he only allowed his fingers to sweep across her buttocks and across her thighs at first, skimming them tantalisingly close to the place she really wanted him to touch.

She writhed in frustration as he stroked her, diverting his touch the second before he reached his ultimate goal. He smiled to himself as she began to scratch her nails into the bark of the tree.

'How about I tease you like this for a while, Emily? Like you've been teasing *me* all afternoon? How would you like that?'

'Theo, please—'

The desperate begging tone of her voice finally broke him, and he slipped his hand under her knickers and slid his fingers over the damp heat between her legs, opening her up to his touch and pushing two fingers easily inside her, her silky arousal allowing him easy entry.

Emily gasped and let out a low, grateful moan, resting her forehead on the tree, rocking back into the motion of his hand.

Moving round her body a little, he slid his other hand down her stomach and into the front of her underwear, bringing his thumb into play, gently circling, then skating over her clitoris, keeping up the steady slide and press with the fingers of his other hand still inside her.

She was trembling now, her breath coming in short, ragged gasps.

He experienced a heady surge of power—something he'd been sadly lacking this afternoon up until this moment.

He felt in control with her at his mercy like this.

She must have already been really keyed up, because barely a moment later she climaxed, letting out a low, guttural groan, her whole body shaking with the force of it.

Sliding his hands away from her, he moved behind her again and leant forward, pressing the hard wall of his chest into her back—making sure to keep the bottom half of himself safely away from her body—feeling her torso rise and fall against his as she struggled to catch her breath.

'Are you satisfied now?' he murmured into her ear. 'You got your orgasm. Now will you stop bugging me?'

'Are you *kidding*?' she groaned, 'You think you can make me come like that and I won't want more? That was masterful.'

His gentle snort made one of the curls that had come loose blow forward across her cheek. 'Thanks for the compliment, but that's all you get.'

Damn the shake in his voice.

'Surely you can't be completely immune to the sexual tension between us?' she muttered. 'You really *would* have to be as hard as stone not to feel it.'

Without warning, she pushed her bottom backwards and pressed it against the now almost painful length of his erection.

'Speaking of hard—'

Before she could twist round and make eye contact with him he stepped swiftly backwards and turned away from her, his shoulders bunched with tension and his fists clenched at his sides.

He needed to get out of there.

'See you on Thursday, Emily,' he forced past a weird tightness in his throat, before striding away.

Damn it, that woman was going to be the death of him.

CHAPTER FOUR

AFTER THEO HAD marched away, Emily tidied herself up and walked back to her car on shaky legs, slumping into the driver's seat in a daze, her whole body still tingling from the incredible orgasm Theo had gifted her.

Never in a million years would she have anticipated *that* happening. After his constant cool rejection of her advances she'd reconciled herself to the fact that she was going to have to put a lot more work into softening him up if she was going to get any kind of reaction out of him.

How wrong she'd been.

It proved to her that he was capable of letting himself go, that there was a deeply sexual man hiding under that reserved veneer, and that he'd been deliberately holding himself back for some reason.

But why? That was the million-dollar question.

He still hadn't kissed her, which made her think he was unwilling to get emotionally involved with her. Using his masterful hands on her clearly didn't count, though.

Luckily for her.

Her body gave a throb of pleasure as she remembered the mind-blowing excitement of the build-up to it, followed swiftly by the intense, out-of-this-world completion she hadn't known was possible.

He'd done something to her—had unearthed something that no other man had even been able to touch.

And she wanted more.

Desperately.

But not today. Today she was going to go home and bask in the memory of it—and the relief of not completely losing her touch with men.

Although Theo's determination not to let her touch him back still bit a little deeper than she liked.

But at least she could congratulate herself on the triumph of making some headway with his mother. She was pretty sure that by the end of dinner on Thursday she'd have the Countess's blessing for Lula's wedding reception to be held here wrapped up tight.

The realisation that this little dance with Theo might be over as soon as that brought her up short. Apart from the regret of perhaps not having enough time to break through his shell, it also suddenly occurred to her that if she was going to utilise the advantage of a relationship with an earl—so the producers of *Treasure Trail* could be made aware of it in time—she needed to act fast.

A whisper in the ear of a friend who worked for one of the gossip magazines should do the trick. She could suggest that a photographer follow her to the house on Thursday, then make sure he had an opportunity to take a good photo of her and Theo acting like lovers.

She was going to have to pull out all the stops for that elusive kiss.

Thursday finally rolled around and Theo woke up feeling relieved that the distracting anticipation of seeing Emily again would be over soon.

He knew he shouldn't have touched her the way he had. It had reminded him too keenly of how he'd used to lose himself in women just like her during those dark days after Hugo had died and he'd lost his way forward, but it had been impossible to stop himself. She seemed to have twisted herself into his control and pulled out the cork.

He'd spent the days between their last meeting and today determinedly trying not to think about her, but the memory of her giving herself so absolutely to him, coming apart so easily under his hands, kept a disturbing erotic tension humming deep inside him.

For those few minutes he'd owned her. He could probably have done anything he'd liked and she would have let him. The memory of having that power over her made him feel rushy with the hunger to exercise it again, but oddly it also produced an aching sort of sadness deep in his belly.

It had been a long time since someone had affected him like that. It hadn't worked out well before and he had a disturbing suspicion that it wouldn't this time either. If he allowed it to go that far.

Which he wouldn't.

He'd promised himself never to allow his feelings about a woman to control him again—even if it was only something as base as lust. He knew from experience that it could quickly morph into something much more dangerous.

And danger was something he could do without right now.

The doorbell rang at seven o'clock on the dot and he gave himself a moment of grace standing behind the door before opening it to her.

This time she'd chosen to wear a figure-hugging dress in a dark green colour that brought out the gold in her eyes. She had on another pair of high heels, and her hair was loose and tamed into a sleek style around her face.

His stomach sank to his knees as he breathed in the familiar sweetly fragrant smell of her, just as the memory of her losing it under his hands came back to hit him full force in the chest.

It was a double whammy he could have done without.

'Hi,' he managed to growl past the sudden tension in his throat.

She was staring at him too, her pupils dilated as if caught in her own saucy reverie.

'Theo. Good to see you again.'

She took a step forward and, putting a hand onto his arm, drew him outside to stand on the stone step with her.

'I wanted to have a quick word before I go in and say hello to your mother,' she said, looking up at him with wide, innocent-looking eyes.

His stomach swooped as he wondered what she was going to say. Was this going to be about what had happened in the wood? Stupidly, he'd hoped they could pretend it hadn't happened and go on as they had before.

Before he'd taken things a step further than he should have.

But of course Emily wasn't the type to ignore something. She was too up-front.

'What is it?' he asked with a frown, in an attempt to discourage the inevitable confrontation.

Clearly she wasn't going to be put off that easily, though, because she slid both hands up over his shoulders in a kind of loose but determined hug.

'I wanted to say thank you for Sunday. I had fun.'

There was a mischievous glint in her eye now.

'Surely after being so…er…*close* like that, I at least qualify for a quick hello kiss now?'

Dropping his gaze to her mouth, he stared at her full lips, which seemed to be coated in some kind of glossy lipstick, and had to steel himself not to pull her against him and kiss her hard.

'Not with that gunk all over your mouth.'

He watched in stupefied awe as she stuck out her tongue and slowly ran it first over her top lip, then her bottom one, taking off the shine but leaving a glistening dampness in its wake.

'Better?' she asked in a low, husky voice that spoke straight to the enormous erection in his trousers.

He cleared his throat and tried to think of something bland and unsexy to kill his maddening reaction. 'I thought I made it clear that Sunday was a one-off. Nothing like that is going to happen again. This is strictly a business arrangement, Emily.'

Her eyebrows rose in defiance. 'You sounded almost regretful there for a moment,' she said, giving him a languid smile. Keeping their gazes locked, she leaned slowly forward to kiss him gently on the cheek, close to his mouth but not quite touching it.

He let it happen, telling himself it would be rude to push her away.

Pulling back, she glanced around her, as if checking for something.

'What's wrong?'

She looked back at him and smiled. 'Nothing. Nothing at all.'

Emily was pretty sure she'd given the photographer hidden in the bushes a good enough opportunity for a shot of the two of them looking all loved up.

She certainly hoped so, because it had almost killed her to act so unconcerned when Theo had rejected her again. She'd brazened it out with a smile, but her insides had sunk low with disappointment at his continued aloofness. It was as if the incident against the tree hadn't happened.

She spent a rather tense dinner, catching Theo alternately giving her frowns or intense stares, which didn't exactly make for a relaxing atmosphere.

In retaliation she touched him as much as she could get away with—on his hand when he passed her the salt, on his thigh when his napkin slid off and she retrieved it for him. She even managed to sweep back a lock of hair which had fallen over his forehead while he was engaged in an involved conversation with his mother about the repair of the heating system in the house.

She thought he was going to stab her with his fork after she performed that one.

Finally they retired to the drawing-room and Theo poured them all drinks before taking the seat on the sofa next to her, his back ramrod-straight and his leg propped on his knee at an angle, so she couldn't sit close to him.

After some beating around the bush, Emily finally managed to turn her conversation with Francesca round to Lula holding her wedding reception at the house again, but was frustrated when the Countess still wouldn't give her a firm commitment.

It was like getting blood out of an icicle.

An hour and one very involved and rather enjoyable conversation about the merits of imprinting young foals later, Emily yawned widely, unable to quell the reflex. She'd not slept well since Sunday and it was catching up with her.

'You look tired, Emily,' Francesca said, raising an eyebrow as if reprimanding her for not looking after herself properly.

Emily hadn't been coddled by a mothering figure in a very long time, and the attentiveness made her feel inexplicably sad.

'I've had a busy few days, Francesca,' she said, beating back the sudden hot, itchy feeling in her eyes.

Francesca frowned. 'Well, you mustn't drive back to London tonight. Stay here and go in the morning. It would be dangerous for you to get into a car in that state.'

She felt Theo tense and shift in the seat next to her and heard him let out a quiet huff of annoyance. Apparently he thought it would be more dangerous for her to stay here.

A fiery rage overtook her, heating her cheeks. She was fed up with him being so unfriendly. Surely it was no skin off his nose if she stayed the night?

'That would be very kind of you, Francesca,' she said, picking up Theo's hand in her hot one and squeezing it hard. 'I could do with being looked after tonight.'

Theo's hand remained rigid in hers.

'That's a good idea,' he said finally, his voice terse and clipped.

'Good, that's settled, then,' Francesca said, rising from her sofa.

Theo stood too. 'Perhaps we should all retire to bed now, as it's so late?'

She knew what he was doing. He was going to bed too so he wasn't left alone with her.

Standing up, she brushed down her dress with hands that were now shaking with indignation. She met his eyes and nodded sharply, flashing him a look of nonchalant defiance. 'Okay. Let's go to bed.'

They walked up the stairs together, with Francesca in the lead and Theo following closely behind. When they reached the top Francesca paused in front of Theo's bedroom door.

'Well, goodnight. I'll see you bright and early for breakfast,' she said, giving them both a cool smile.

She paused, seemingly waiting for something.

There was a tense silence as they all looked at each other.

'Goodnight, Mother,' Theo said finally, opening the door to his room.

Francesca still didn't move.

Theo gave her another second to go to her own room, and when she didn't made a small huffing noise and disappeared through his doorway.

Emily gave Francesca a tight smile and a small clumsy wave before following Theo in and closing the door behind her.

She found him standing by the bed with his arms folded tightly against his chest.

'What?' she said, flinging her hands wide. 'What did you expect me to do? Drive all the way back to London in a dangerously tired state? Or are you angry with me for not insisting on being taken to a guest bedroom? Don't you think that would have looked weird, considering we're supposed to be so in love? She was waiting for me to come in here like it was a test or something. I had to.'

He relaxed his arms and sighed, sweeping a hand over his brow, then through his hair.

When he looked back at her his eyes were tired. 'Fair point.'

'Honestly, Theo, what do you think I am? Some desperate groupie who just can't function without your attention?' She decided not to let herself dwell on the undertone of that question. 'Because I have my own life, you know. I have lots of friends in London and I could find myself some company any night of the week if I wanted to.'

'I know that, Emily, and it's not what I was implying.'

'Really? 'Cos it sure felt like it.'

They glared at each other, neither of them seemingly willing to give in.

Theo broke first. 'Look, I apologise. I've not been sleeping well and it's affected my judgement.'

She raised an eyebrow. 'You've not been sleeping well either?'

'No.'

'Why not?'

He didn't answer at first, just looked at her with those intensely moody green eyes of his. 'I don't know,' he said finally.

Her stomach sank. She'd been desperate for him to say something else, and she didn't like the way that made her feel.

The hot pressure was back behind her eyes again. She really must be tired if she was letting him get to her like this.

'Look, I'll wait on that armchair in the corner for ten minutes, then I'll sneak off to one of the guest bedrooms,' she said.

'Don't be ridiculous. My mother might catch you. Just get into bed, Emily,' he ordered, his voice low and gruff.

She stared at him in defiance for a moment, before accepting that he was right and it wasn't worth the risk. 'Okay. Fine. Do you have a T-shirt I can borrow? I don't want to sleep in my dress.'

'Yes.'

He disappeared into his dressing room and came back with a soft-looking black cotton T-shirt.

'I'll use the bathroom first so you can change in privacy,' he said, not waiting for her response before striding out of the room.

She sighed and sat down on the edge of the bed, her legs feeling strangely wobbly. How the heck was she going to be able to sleep? Her heart was already thumping like a jackhammer and it was only going to get worse when she was enveloped in the heat and scent of his bed, with him lying *right there* next to her.

Undressing fully for comfort, she pulled on the T-shirt he'd given her, realising too late that it smelt of the washing powder he used on his clothes. It was pure *Essence of Theo.*

He came back a minute later, knocking gently on the bathroom door to warn her, before striding back in in a pair of sleep shorts, his chest bare.

Trying not to let herself gawp at the sight of his broad, toned torso, she excused herself and went and got washed in the en-suite too, using the new toothbrush he'd put out for her.

Staring at herself in the mirror, she willed herself to keep it together. It would be okay, sleeping in the same bed with him, even if she *was* shaking all over from the effort of keeping from either slapping him or jumping on him.

She wasn't going to give him the satisfaction of seeing just how much he was messing with her head with his hot and cold behaviour.

Returning to the bedroom, she found him already in bed, the duvet just covering his lower torso as he read one of the paperbacks she'd spied in his drawer the first time she'd been in this room.

She got into bed next to him and fluffed up the pillows to her satisfaction before settling back into them.

'Comfortable?' he said, with a glint of humour in his eyes.

The sudden switch from gruffness to jokey camaraderie made her even more nervous. It was easier to deal with his presence right there next to her when she was annoyed with him.

'Yes, thank you,' she replied casually, smoothing the duvet down around her and staring up at the ceiling, desperately trying to ignore the low throb of arousal that just *wouldn't die* whenever he was in her vicinity.

He leant over to his bedside table, dropping the book onto it before flicking off the lamp and plunging the room into darkness.

It took a minute or so for her eyes to adjust, and she glanced across at him to find he was staring up at the ceiling too. She shifted a little, to get a bit more comfortable, and felt him do the same beside her.

After a few more minutes of restless wriggling she forced herself to lie still and willed her tense muscles to relax. Theo's breathing sounded measured and shallow, as if he was drifting off to sleep, and she cursed him for not being even slightly affected by her being there. What *was* it with this guy? He seemed to have an iron-clad will with a Kevlar coating.

Squeezing her eyes shut, she tried to blank her mind of him. But memories of the incident against the tree insistently crept back into her thoughts and she squirmed as heat rushed between her legs, intensifying the deep, pounding ache of need already there.

Letting out a frustrated sigh, she turned over to face the middle of the bed and found Theo only inches away, his eyes open, looking at her with intense concentration, as if he was trying to rein something in. They stared at each other through the gloom and she realised that his breathing wasn't steady and relaxed at all. It was short and ragged. Just like hers.

That perpetual frown was on his face again, and instinctively she reached out a hand to touch him there, to see if she could somehow rub it away.

He moved quickly, grabbing her wrist, then rolling over her, pinning her arm against the bed by her head. Then, when she stubbornly tried to touch him with her other hand, he grabbed it and pinned that one too, until she was trapped under him.

His body was heavy and hard against hers, and she could feel his chest rising and falling rapidly in time with her own. He was staring into her eyes again, his mouth only centimetres away from hers. His scent was all around her, clean and fresh and intoxicating.

She begged him with her eyes to close the gap and finally kiss her; to relieve the throbbing, yawning ache that had plagued her since he'd last touched her.

Something flickered in his eyes, as if he was having an internal fight with himself, and she cheered the devil in him on, willing him to win and let go, to ravish her lips with his—and then her body. Her hot, trembling, lust-addled body.

For a moment she truly thought he was going to do it, but at the last second his scowl deepened and he drew away from her mouth, moving his head downwards. She nearly shouted out in frustration.

Until she felt his mouth on her neck.

His lips were firm and warm on her skin. Sparks of pure joy radiated out from where they pressed against her and twists of pleasure wound through the rest of her body, pooling heavily in the yearning space between her legs.

Releasing her captured arms, he moved his hands down to find the hem of the T-shirt she was wearing and slid it up her body, groaning low in his throat as he realised she wasn't wearing any underwear. Pulling away from her for a moment, he ripped the T-shirt up over her head and flung it away from them, returning quickly to cover one of her nipples with his mouth, biting down gently on the swollen bud, causing her to push her pelvis up off the bed towards him as her whole body responded to the erotic bite.

Moving her hands to grasp his shoulders, she was shocked when he abruptly stopped teasing her breast with his teeth and pulled her hands off him, pushing them back down against the bed again.

'No,' he growled, clearly unwilling for her to lead things at all.

He wanted her totally at his mercy. The thought only increased the insistent ache in her.

While she found it frustrating not to get involved, she wasn't about to make him stop. So she left her arms where he'd pushed them, biting her lip as he moved on to give the same attention to her other breast before making his way down her belly with firm licks and kisses.

He skirted the place she most wanted his mouth and she heard herself give deep, involuntary groans as he kissed down her thighs, then back up, to skim over the aching centre of her and drop kisses against her hipbones. Moving further down the bed, he slid his hands under the backs of her thighs and pushed up, positioning her legs so they sat crooked over his shoulders.

He paused for what felt like days, his mouth hovering over the place she wanted his attention, his breath hot on her skin.

She lost her cool. 'Dammit, Theo, if you don't get your mouth on me right now I'm going to go crazy,' she yelped, surprising herself with the force of the demand.

He didn't give in right away, just let her squirm beneath him—until finally, *finally*, he rewarded her with a long, firm lick against the most needy part of her. The relief was exquisite—like diving into a cool pool of water on a stiflingly hot day—and she shouted out in triumph, her shout soon turning to pants of ecstasy as he continued to lick and suck her.

He brought his hands into play, catching a sweet spot with his fingers that increased the intensity of the sensation, heightening the heady pressure that rapidly built inside her, closer and closer, until he finally took her over the edge. She screwed her face up as the orgasm hit, racking her body with the most intense waves of pleasure she'd ever experienced, and she heard low, guttural moans that she barely recognised as her own coming from deep in her throat.

Once the aftermath of pleasure had finally receded she lay staring up at the ceiling, her mouth open in shock and awe as she tried to process what had just happened.

Theo had moved away from her and was now lying on his back in the bed next to her, staring up at the ceiling too.

Rolling onto her side, she reached out to touch his chest. But he caught her hand and gently but firmly pushed it away.

'Why, Theo? Why won't you let me touch you? I want to make you feel good too,' she whispered, the sting of the rejection making her voice ragged.

'Because I don't want you to.' His voice was curt, but she was pretty sure she heard an underlying shake to it.

'But why not?'

'I don't want to talk about it, Emily. Leave it alone.'

'What happened to you?' she asked, reaching out a hand to touch his shoulder.

He shrugged her off, moving closer to the edge of the bed, away from her.

'I said I don't want to talk about it. Go to sleep,' he said, turning over so his back was to her.

Staring at his rigid body, she flashed back to those moments when he'd hovered his mouth over hers, giving her palpitations at the awareness that she might finally be allowed to kiss him. In those few fuzzy seconds she'd hoped she'd somehow broken through his wall of steel, but then he'd moved away, denying her the pleasure of his surrender.

It was exhausting, dealing with his yo-yoing changes of mind.

An overwhelming tiredness overtook her and she yawned. Amazingly, it seemed that even the mystery of his constant rejection wasn't enough to keep her awake right at that moment.

Pulling the covers up over her head, she curled her knees into her chest, still acutely aware of the aftershocks of her orgasm that warmed her body, and let her thoughts drift away.

She'd figure it out in the morning.

Theo woke early the next day, with Emily's hair tickling his nose. She'd somehow managed to wriggle next to him in the night, and was tucked inside the scoop of his body, her shapely backside pressed against his bent thighs.

After he'd been sure she'd fallen asleep last night he'd got up and taken a freezing cold shower, only managing to take the edge off his fierce burning need to bury himself inside her and have done with it. But he knew if he took a step over the line he'd drawn for himself that would be it—there'd be no going back.

Not that he hadn't already nudged right up to it by going down on her, but he figured if he kept her satisfied he'd be able to get through this thing unscathed.

And it hadn't exactly been an arduous chore. She had an incredible body—one he'd enjoyed kissing and licking and feeling squirm beneath him immensely.

There was still something about her that made him jumpy, though; he sensed a deeply buried secret which she used her overwhelming personality to hide. Something dark, hidden deep. There had to be. No one could be that upbeat and carefree for real. She had to be masking something.

Not that he cared enough to find out what it was.

Getting up, being careful not to wake her, he got dressed and made his way downstairs.

He found his mother already in the kitchen, reading the papers and drinking weak tea.

'Good morning, Theo,' she said, looking up from what she was reading to give him an assessing glance. 'You look as though you haven't slept all night.'

Was that a glint of mischief in her eyes? Surely not. His mother didn't have the verve for mischief.

'I'm fine,' he said, going over to the counter to set up the coffee-maker.

When he turned back she was watching him with a discerning look in her eye. She got up gracefully from the table and walked over to where he was standing.

'I'm going for a walk and I may not be back before Emily leaves. Would you tell her that I've made my decision?' she said, pausing for effect.

'Yes, of course,' he said, to fill the irritating nerve-filled gap she'd left.

'I'd be happy for her friend to hold her wedding reception here,' she said, placing a hand onto his shoulder in an uncharacteristic show of affection.

It took him a moment to get over the shock of her

touching him before he was able to respond. 'She'll be delighted.'

'Good—good. Thank you, darling. See you later for lunch,' she said, before sweeping out of the room.

He stood there, staring at the empty kitchen, feeling a strange mixture of relief and something else he couldn't quite place. Disappointment, perhaps? Because his mother's agreement spelt the end of Emily's need to be here, and he didn't quite know how to feel about that any more.

He wanted to get back to work without constantly being distracted by the thought of her, but he also accepted that she'd be leaving a niggling hole behind once she was gone from his life.

Clearly he'd got a little too reliant on the anticipation of Emily turning up to disrupt his day with her forthright teasing and game playing.

She'd changed the rules on him.

It was time to release her from their agreement.

CHAPTER FIVE

AFTER EMILY HAD got up and found the bed empty of Theo she made her way downstairs and discovered him alone in the kitchen, drinking coffee and reading one of the many newspapers strewn all over the large oak table.

'Good morning,' she said, suddenly a little jumpy at the sight of him. He looked tired—as if he hadn't slept at all. Perhaps he should have accepted her offer of an orgasm in return—that would have knocked him right out, just as it had her.

'You get the newspapers?' she said, walking up to the table and rifling through them to see which ones he chose to read. They were mostly broadsheets. 'That's so old school. You're the only person our age I know who still reads the news off real paper. You know there's this thing called *the Internet*, right? It's a fount of information.'

He ignored her jibe. 'Help yourself to coffee,' he said, waving towards the machine on the counter without looking up.

She went over to it and poured herself a mug full of the hot liquid nectar, then sat down at the table next to him. Her body appeared to be throbbing with the pleasurable memory of how he'd touched and kissed her last night, and she was keen to reconnect with him this morning. Just in case there was a chance of second helpings.

'Where's your mother?' she asked.

'She went out for a walk.'

Emily nodded, pleased they wouldn't be interrupted. She had this strange yearning to spend a bit of time with Theo in the daylight, and she didn't fancy having his mother playing gooseberry to it. If truth be told, she'd got on quite well with the woman since they'd got past their frosty start, but it would be a real mood-killer to have to hang around with Francesca all day today.

'So you did it,' he said, finally looking up from his paper.

He sat back in his chair and wrapped his hands around his mug before raising it to his lips and taking a long sip.

She waited impatiently for him to continue. 'Did what?' she blurted, barely a couple of seconds later. She'd never been good at waiting for news.

'My mother's agreed to let Lula use the house for her wedding reception.'

He gave her a minute to punch the air repeatedly with joy, before looking at her pointedly, demanding her attention back.

'I think she's convinced enough of our relationship now,' he said, placing the mug carefully down on the table. 'We don't need to hammer it any more. In fact we'd probably be tempting fate by arranging more *dates* around her. We're bound to let something slip if we start to relax and get too cocky.'

His blunt suggestion felt like a smack in the face after the closeness they'd shared only hours ago. Obviously Theo didn't have as much of a problem with cutting their little dalliance short as she did. He'd pulled any trace of the passion from last night tightly back under wraps—she was now beginning to think she must have dreamt it.

The guy was phenomenal at detachment. He even

gave *her* a run for her money, and that was really saying something.

She got up, feeling a sudden urge to move about. She hated dealing with things ending. This was precisely why she never let herself get too attached to a man.

'Okay, then I'd better head off. I guess I'll see you in a few weeks at Lula's wedding,' she said smartly, making for the door.

'Emily?' His voice was gruff, with a hint of urgency.

She stopped and turned to face him again, her heart pounding, wondering whether he was going to change his mind and ask her to stay for just a little bit longer.

'It was fun working with you,' he said, before giving her a curt nod and turning back to his newspaper.

She was well and truly dismissed.

She wasn't going to let him get to her.

No way.

When she got home she took a shower, then went straight out again to see some friends, ending up having a fun, raucous day with them which was only marginally tainted by a nagging sense that something was missing.

It couldn't have been Theo, though—she was sure of that.

He called a couple of days later to let her know that he'd managed to persuade the vicar of the estate's chapel to let Lula and Tristan get married there if they wanted.

'That's fantastic, Theo!'

There was a short silence on the other end of the line. 'Yes. Well, he seemed quite happy to accommodate a good friend of the family.'

She got the impression Theo had been given the third degree about his own plans for getting married in the future. That must have made him uncomfortable.

'Well, Lula will be delighted when I tell her. It'll be the icing on the wedding cake.'

'Good,' he said brusquely.

There was another pause. 'So, how's it going with your mother? Is she still there?' she asked, to fill the descending silence.

'Actually, I need to talk to you about that.'

Dead air hummed through the line as she waited for him to continue, her heart-rate picking up and her hand twitching around the phone in anticipation of what he might be about to say.

'Yeeess…?'

She told herself to keep cool, annoyed by the disturbing hum of excitement in her belly provoked by his cryptic silence.

'She's going to stay with friends while Lula's wedding is going on at the house and for a few days afterwards, so all the rooms are free for the guests, but then she's coming back to stay for another week. She's—' he took a breath '—keen to see you again. She wants me to set up another lunch date. She intimated that she'd be going back to Spain soon after that, and that she's been considering reinstating my inheritance and signing the house over to me before she leaves.'

Emily felt a smug smile pull at her lips and was glad he couldn't see her through the phone line. 'I see. So you still need me, then?' she said, forcing as much nonchalance into her tone as she could muster.

He cleared his throat, the sound rumbling down the phone line at her. 'It would seem so, yes.'

'Your mother seems to have taken a real shine to me in fact.'

'She does.'

'Well, fancy that.' She couldn't keep the glee out of her voice this time.

'So, will you consider it?' He was clearly trying hard to keep his irritation tamped down.

It was her turn to leave a long pause this time, and she listened to his breathing quicken as she bit her tongue to stop herself from speaking.

'Okay, Theo, since you went to the trouble of securing the chapel for Lula, I'd be happy to come to one more lunch with your mother,' she said finally.

She caught his short exhalation of breath before he spoke. 'Thank you, Emily, I appreciate it.'

'You're welcome.'

Another pause.

'Okay, good,' she said to fill the gap. 'Well, I'll see you at the wedding then.'

'No, you won't. I don't *attend* the weddings. I let my events manager take care of all that.'

Disappointment trickled down into her stomach but she ignored it. It didn't matter that she wouldn't be seeing him then. In fact it would be better not to be distracted on Lula's big day.

'Oh, right. Okay, then.'

'I'll be in touch afterwards to arrange the lunch date. Once you've had time to recover.'

'Righto.'

'So, I'll speak to you soon.'

'Sure,' she replied, moments before he cut the line.

She stared at the silent phone for a long minute, trying to relax her baffled smile.

That had excited her a lot more than it should have done.

Two days later the photo of the two of them canoodling outside Theo's house appeared in her friend's gossip mag and she got another phone call from him—only this time not such a positive one.

'How the *hell* did the gutter press find out about us?' he growled, as soon as she'd picked up his call.

Her heart gave a little flutter of unease. 'Er…well, I *might* have mentioned something to Lula about having dinner at your house, and it's possible she *might* have let it slip in conversation with a friend of ours who's a journalist.'

She crossed her fingers and mentally apologised to Lula for the lie at her expense. She knew her friend would take the heat for her if she needed her to, though. They had a long-standing agreement regarding men and dates.

'That's a lot of mights, Emily.'

'Look, I'm sorry. I understand why you'd be angry—because they came onto your property and spied on a private moment—but I can't see how it can be a bad thing generally. In fact if your mother gets to see it or hear about it it'll only cement her faith in our deeply committed relationship.'

He let out a grunt of reluctant agreement.

'I think you look amazing in the photo, by the way. Very manly,' she said, hoping a bit of sweet-talk would appease him. Not that he'd ever shown any sign of caring about how he looked, but she'd found it was always worth applying a bit of flattery to a situation.

There was silence on the other end.

'Are you still there?' she asked.

'Yes,' he ground out. 'Listen to me, Emily. I do *not* want to get caught up in the media circus you seem to inhabit. If I see any more pictures of the two of us in the papers I'm going to seriously reconsider whether Lula can hold her reception at my house. Do you understand?'

She swallowed hard. 'Yes.'

'I don't want to have to start locking my gates.'

'Understood.'

'So we're clear?'

'As ice.' She took a steadying breath, feeling the need to exert some damage control. 'Look, don't worry about that story,' she said, crossing her fingers even harder. 'It'll be tomorrow's fish and chip wrapper.'

'It had better be,' he said, not sounding at all placated.

'Okay. Well, I guess I'll speak to you after the wedding.'

'Yes,' he said, and cut the call.

The guy seriously needed some lessons in charm.

Emily spent the next week at Lula's house, attempting to keep her friend from going crazy in the run-up to her wedding day—which was lucky as it took her mind off Theo for a bit. She'd never been so preoccupied with a man and it was shaking her up something chronic.

It was time to face facts, though. It was clear that he wasn't interested in taking their seriously messed-up connection any further and she was going to have to chalk it up to experience and move on.

The day of the wedding dawned and Emily wondered whether she was actually more nervous about it than Lula.

After weeks of flapping about, her friend now appeared to be in a state of otherworldly serenity—as if she'd reconciled herself to the fact that there was nothing else she could do about the arrangements for the day and was determined to enjoy every minute of it.

Ironically, they were using Theo's bedroom to get changed into their wedding garb, and Emily couldn't help but repeatedly glance at the bed and remember what had happened in it only two weeks ago. It all felt like a dream now. A very intense, erotic dream.

'So what's going on with Theo now?' Lula asked as she applied a second coat of mascara to her lashes with a steady hand.

Her friend looked utterly stunning in an ivory Grecian-style wedding dress, with her long hazelnut-brown hair twisted up into an amazingly complex hairdo of plaits and twists that would have made any engineer scratch his head in questioning wonder.

Emily shrugged. 'Nothing, really.'

Lula turned away from the mirror and shot her a worried look. 'Oh, no! I thought you two were getting on really well?'

Realising her friend needed to hear happy news to maintain her bubble of calm, Emily backtracked quickly. 'I mean I haven't caught up with him recently, what with hanging out with you in the run-up to today, but who knows? He's a great guy.'

Lula beamed at her, clearly caught up in her dreamy world of romance. 'He must be incredible in bed to have kept your interest this long.'

'I wouldn't know—we haven't gone all the way,' Emily muttered, trying to keep the touchiness out of her voice and her gaze from shooting towards his large bed.

'Ah, so *that's* the attraction? He's keeping you at arm's length? Wow. That's a new one.'

Emily snorted, but decided to let Lula keep her fantasy that she was involved in an exciting build-up to a torrid affair with him. Her friend was such a die-hard romantic, but far be it for her to mock her views on love and relationships on her wedding day.

'Do you think he might be The One?' Lula asked innocently, her big blue eyes wide with hope.

This time Emily couldn't keep back the splutter of disdain.

'Don't be daft, Lu, you know I'm not into all that *destiny* stuff.'

Lula eyed her sadly. 'Yeah, maybe...but you shouldn't be so quick to dismiss it.'

Emily flapped a dismissive hand at her friend. 'Not everyone needs what you and Tristan have.'

'I know that. I'm just worried that you're denying yourself something amazing without realising how good it could be for you.'

Emily just gave her friend a placating smile, hoping she'd drop the subject soon. It was making her uncomfortable.

'Please tell me you at least *like* him,' Lula pressed, clearly not reading her *drop it* signals today. 'The romantic in me needs to hear it,' she said, batting her eyelashes.

Emily grinned at her friend's determination. 'Actually, I *do* like him. He has this brooding, angry appeal. He's quite something. *Veeery* sexy.'

'Good. Then give him a chance, Em,' she said, turning back to the mirror to apply another coat of lipstick.

Emily caught her snort before it escaped. Unfortunately that was easier said than done.

Theo kept a low profile during the wedding, spending his time either in the workshop or the guesthouse, attempting to keep Emily's unnerving presence out of his mind.

He couldn't quite bring himself to believe that if he *did* give in to his urges she wouldn't turn around and start demanding more than just sex from him.

It wasn't worth the risk.

He was still a little suspicious, too, about the picture of the two of them together in that misleading pose—but then what did he know about modern celebrities and the invasion of their privacy?

Nothing.

What he did know was that he sure as hell didn't want to get caught up in it.

Emily was clearly a one-way ticket to Troublesville, and that was a place he really didn't want to visit again. In fact, come to think of it, he'd bet his life she was causing some kind of chaos over at his house today. Perhaps making a smart-alecky comment to the wrong person and causing a fist-fight, or dancing on his mahogany dining table in her stilettos.

The more he thought about it, the more apprehensive he felt about what exactly was going on over there.

Perhaps he should go over and have a very quick check that everything was okay. His events manager had agreed to run this wedding for him, after he'd given her a large bonus on top of her regular fee for the trouble his mother had caused, so he was confident that the arrangements were going as planned, but he told himself he should make a cursory check anyway.

It was his duty as caretaker of the house.

Dumping the book he'd unsuccessfully been attempting to read on the coffee table, he took a quick shower and got dressed in a pair of smart trousers and a shirt and strode over to the house, which was now lit up brilliantly against the growing dusk of the evening.

Walking through the smartly dressed crowd of guests, he craned his neck to see whether he could locate the bride—on the pretext of offering his congratulations on her marriage and getting feedback on how the house had worked as a venue for it—only to catch sight of Emily, entertaining a crowd of people next to the large stone fireplace in the drawing-room.

He stopped dead, his heart hammering in his chest and his breath quickening in his lungs as he stared at her.

She looked utterly beautiful, in an elegant vibrant red strapless dress that looked incredible against the dark colour of her hair. As he watched her laughing and joking with the other guests he felt all the times he'd caught himself smiling in the last week—remembering something funny or smart she'd said—come rushing back to him, and he had to forcibly stop himself from striding over there to listen in to the story she was regaling her audience with.

His whole body throbbed with the control he had to exercise over it.

Don't do it, Theo, it's not worth it.

Someone put a gentle hand on his arm, making him start, and he tore his eyes away from Emily to see a short, pretty woman smiling up at him, swaying slightly on her heels as if high on champagne and joy. Judging by the fact she was wearing a wedding dress, he guessed this must be Lula.

'Lord Berkeley?'

'Theo,' he corrected her distractedly.

She smiled. 'I wanted to come over and thank you for letting Tristan and I use your beautiful house for our wedding. You know, I used to live in the nearby village and I passed this house every day on the bus on the way to school. I had whimsical dreams about getting married here for years. It seemed like such a romantic place.' She tightened her grip on his arm, squeezing it in gratitude before letting go. 'Thank you so much for making it happen.'

He nodded. 'It was all down to Emily, actually. She's the one who persuaded my mother to change her mind. I'm sorry, by the way, for causing you the stress of thinking you had to find somewhere else at such short notice. I had no idea my mother had done it until I got home to an answer machine full of distressed messages. The woman's a law unto herself.'

Lula glanced over to where Emily stood, entertaining the crowd gathered around her with another tale that made them all laugh as one. 'You know, I don't think I've ever seen Emily more buzzed than when she was coming here to have dinner with you.' She leaned in conspiratorially, widening her blue eyes at him in a beseeching manner. 'She's had a pretty tough life and she deserves some happiness.'

He gave her a stiff smile, uncomfortable at Lula's implication that it should be *him* making her happy. 'Funny—that's what she says about you.'

Her returning smile was warm. 'Yeah, we're both a bit messed up in our own special ways. Parents eh, who'd have 'em?'

'I'm with you on that one.'

He nodded to punctuate the end of the conversation and turned to walk away, but Lula put her hand back on his arm to stop him.

'Look, I know she can come across as a bit of a handful, but she's a good person—the most fiercely loyal, kind and caring person I've ever met—and if you've made it into the small circle of people she cares about you should congratulate yourself. She doesn't trust people easily. Not after what happened with her mother.' She let out a low, sad-sounding breath. 'It's no wonder she doesn't ever want to see her again after what she had to go through.'

He went suddenly cold, and a heavy feeling slid uncomfortably into his stomach. 'I thought her mother was dead?'

Colour flooded across Lula's cheeks and her gaze shot

away from his, as if she'd realised that she'd said something she shouldn't have.

'Lula?'

'I just mean…I'm surprised she talked about her mother at all. It's not a subject you can get her to discuss very easily,' she mumbled, still not looking at him.

'That's not what you meant, Lula. It sounded like you said she wasn't dead. Is she alive?'

Lula's face was now beet-red. 'I shouldn't have—' She shook her head, her eyes wild. 'Em's going to kill me!'

'Tell me what's going on, Lula.' He realised his tone was gruff, but he needed to know what he was up against here. If Emily had lied to him about her mother being dead, what else had she lied about?

Lula's shoulders sagged and she gave him a pained look from under her lashes. 'I shouldn't have told you that. She doesn't want other people to know about—things.'

'So her mother's *alive*, then?' This was like getting sludge out of an engine.

Lula was staring at the floor now, and when she answered her voice was so quiet he only just caught the word.

'Yes.'

His chest tightened with unease. 'Why did she lie to me?'

Lula shook her head, still staring down. 'You should ask *her* that. I think I've done enough damage already. My lips are now sealed.' She looked up at him and drew a finger across her mouth as if to zip it.

He let out a breath, trying to keep his frustration out of his body language. 'Okay.'

It wasn't fair to put Lula through an interrogation on her wedding day, and from the shuttered look on her face he didn't think she'd be giving anything else away anyway.

'Well, congratulations on your marriage. I'm really pleased the house worked for you as a venue,' he said, then nodded curtly at her and walked out of the room before Emily caught sight of him.

Leaving the festive atmosphere humming behind him, he went and paced around in the cool air of the garden for a while, turning over the information he'd just heard in his mind. He felt uneasy and restless. Why would Emily lie to him like that? What was she hiding?

He had no idea, and it was probably better not to know.

After a bit more pacing he decided to make a quick trip to the kitchen and fetch a bottle of whisky from the larder to take back to the guesthouse with him, before settling in there for the night.

The image of Emily in her red dress, her expression alive with laughter, played round and round his head as he pushed through the crowd of people towards the kitchen. He prayed he wasn't going to bump into her. He didn't know whether he'd be able to keep his cool with the knowledge that she'd been lying to him firmly embedded in the front of his mind.

Sighing, he ran a hand through his hair. He was definitely in need of the numbing effects of alcohol tonight.

As he walked down the hallway towards the kitchen he thought he could hear raised voices coming from that direction and picked up his pace, his heart thumping in his chest as he recognised Emily's voice.

Striding into the room, he was alarmed to find a small group of people watching Emily in bemusement as she pointed a shaking finger in a man's face while he stood there with a contrite expression on his face, his arms folded defensively in front of him and a coat grasped in his hand.

'I can't *believe* you'd try and sneak off early from your own daughter's wedding!' she was yelling at him, her face flushed with anger and her eyes wild.

The man's expression morphed into a sneer. 'I really don't think it's your place to tell *me* how to behave, Emily.'

'What the hell are you talking about?' she shot back.

'Considering your *loose* reputation, I don't think you have any right to be taking the moral high ground.'

Theo frowned, riled on Emily's behalf to hear her spoken to like that. She might be a little wild, according to the reports he'd read about her in the press, but she wasn't a marriage-wrecker or a gold-digger.

'What I choose to do with my life has absolutely nothing to do with you,' she replied, her voice now shaking with anger.

Lula's father took a step towards Emily. 'It affects me when it's *my* daughter you're leading astray.'

He leaned in closer to her, but Theo was pleased to see she steadfastly refused to move, her expression remaining defiant.

'At least I'm here, celebrating with my family. Where are *your* family, Emily? From what I've heard they don't even acknowledge you. Your father certainly doesn't have a good word to say about you.'

'Leave my family out of this,' she said quietly, her tone edged with steel.

'Why should I? You seem quite happy to muscle into mine.'

'I'm not muscling in. Lula chose me to be her bridesmaid. I think you'll find I'm more like family to her than you are.'

Lula's father let out a sharp bark of laughter. 'If you were part of *my* family I'd be ashamed to admit it to anyone.'

Before Theo could react, Emily marched right up to Lula's father until she was almost nose to nose with him. 'You're a pathetic excuse for a father,' she spat into his face, sending the man reeling back in shock. 'And don't you *ever* speak to me like that again!' she said, more quietly this time, her voice wobbling with emotion and her eyes glistening with angry tears.

Something twisted hard in Theo's gut and he stepped forward and put a hand on her arm, guiding her behind him as Lula's father turned on her with balled fists and an expression of pure rage on his face.

'You little b—'

'I think it's time for you to leave the room,' Theo said forcefully to the man, acutely aware of Emily trembling under his grip.

Lula's father let out a disgusted snort and without another word strode out of the kitchen, his tense shoulder banging against Theo's in his haste to leave.

'You're a selfish bastard!' Emily shouted after him.

Her eyes were blazing with the fire Theo admired so much in her.

She swivelled to face him. 'What are you doing? I was handling things fine by myself, Theo,' she said, turning her ire on him now.

'Yeah, it looked like it,' he said, shaking his head at her.

'What do you want?' she asked, pulling at her arm to try and release his hold on her.

He held her fast. 'Not here,' he said, tightening his grip and guiding her firmly out of the room.

He didn't know why, but that moment of vulnerability

she'd shown right before he'd stepped in had him rattled. It was the first time he'd seen her let her guard down, and against his better judgement it made him want to dig deeper.

'What? Are you going to tell me off for making a scene in your house now?' she muttered, dragging her feet as he walked her into the empty library, her bag knocking against his thigh as it swung from her shoulder.

He let go of her so he could shut and lock the door behind them, then turned to face her again.

'He had it coming, Theo! He's never been there for Lula and I wasn't about to let him slope away, thinking it was okay to treat her with so little respect on her wedding day.'

'I don't care about that, Emily,' he said quietly.

She stilled and looked at him with fierce eyes. 'Then what do you want?'

'I want to know why you've been lying to me about your mother being dead.'

CHAPTER SIX

ALL THE FIGHT seemed to drain right out of her and her shoulders slumped. 'Lula told you?' she asked quietly, her brows drawing together and her chin dropping an inch or two.

'Accidentally,' he said, folding his arms across his chest.

She shrugged, but maintained eye contact. 'Yeah, well, it didn't seem to matter since it wasn't a real relationship. Who cares if I've told a little white lie to keep myself protected?'

He dropped his arms to his sides as his heart gave a weird stutter in his chest. 'I care.'

She took a deliberate step forward and stared at him defiantly, seemingly coming back to life. 'Why?'

He stared back, his thoughts lost in memories of them together, here at the house: of his irritation with her for being so pushy and forcing him to the edge of his comfort zone, of him not being able to stop himself from touching her, then more recently of aching like crazy to get back the compelling camaraderie that had developed between them despite his best efforts to keep himself aloof from her.

Dropping his gaze to her mouth, he was surprised to see that her lower lip was trembling.

He stared at it, unable to look away.

Almost in a trance, he raised his hand and brushed the pad of his thumb over her lip, feeling her open her mouth a fraction under the pressure of his touch, then the gentle slick sweep of her tongue as she ran it against the tip.

Heat flared through his body and he jerked his hand away from her and looked into her eyes, seeing the same hunger he was feeling reflected right back at him. And then suddenly he was kissing her, and all the anger and passion and pain that he'd kept in check for so long poured out of him and into the connection their mouths made. Except it was more than just kissing. It was a fight for supremacy. He wanted her to feel him in every way possible, to overpower every molecule of her.

She kissed him back, winding her arms around his back and pressing herself tightly against his body. Her lips were soft and warm against his and he slipped his tongue into her mouth to taste the sweetness of her, revelling in the relief of finally allowing himself the pleasure.

She pulled back to stare at him, her eyes wide and stunned. 'You kissed me!'

'I did,' he muttered, going in for another kiss, feeling a yearning ache to connect with her again.

'But you don't kiss women you don't care about,' she murmured against his mouth.

He growled low in his throat. 'Shut up, Emily, okay? Just shut up.'

And then he kissed her hard again, owning her mouth with his, taking what he wanted from her. And she let him. But it wasn't enough—he wanted more.

Backing her against the desk in the middle of the room, he ran his hands down the sides of her dress, bunching the silky material in his hands and hoisting it upwards until he found the hem. Pushing her back, he forced her to sit on the desk, pushing her legs apart so he could stand between them and slide his hand between her thighs, up to the apex of her legs to find the barrier of her knickers.

She wasn't wearing any.

'What is it with you and no underwear?' he groaned, feeling his erection pressing hard against the constricting material of his trousers.

'They were ruining the line of my dress,' she muttered, her voice harsh with lust.

She gasped and moaned low in her throat as he teased his fingers against her, then slid them into her slick, waiting warmth, glancing his thumb over her clitoris as he went.

He kissed her again and felt her reach for the button on his trousers, popping it open without much effort and sliding down the zip so she could get her hand into his boxers and free him from the prison of his trousers.

He swore under his breath as her firm touch encircled the hard length of him and he pushed into her grip, desperate for her to relieve the almost painful ache of his arousal. Their kissing was fierce now, uncontrolled and messy. They rocked against each other, both gasping air into their lungs, their bodies moving closer and closer together.

He felt her fumble at her side with her other hand, then release her hold on him while she opened up the bag she'd been carrying to rummage around inside it.

Pulling away from her in protest at the loss of her touch, he realised she had a condom in her hand.

'I see you were prepared for this happening,' he muttered, sliding his hand from between her thighs as unease began to penetrate through the haze of lust.

'I'm always ready for anything,' she said, and grabbed

hold of him again, stroking up and down his hard shaft, giving a little twist at the end which had him sucking a harsh breath in through his teeth.

So what if she carried condoms? he asked himself as lust won him over again. If she hadn't things would be slowing down right now instead of heating up. He should be grateful, because now he'd allowed himself to leap over the line he *really* didn't want to have to turn back.

Groaning low in his throat, he grabbed the condom from her and tore it open, then slid back out of her hold so he could sheath himself with fumbling fingers.

Once he was satisfied with the fit he recaptured her mouth and leaned over her, steadying himself against the desk with one hand as he guided himself into her with the other. She gasped as he pushed deep, and he felt her open up to take his length.

And then he began to thrust, unable to control the urge to move, keep moving, keep feeling. And she encouraged him, leaning back and pulling him with her.

Bracing himself against the table, he pounded inside her, hard and fast, pushing her higher up the smooth surface, and she wrapped her legs around his back and clung on, riding the movement with him.

Squeezing his eyes shut, he let himself go, giving her everything he had until he heard her cry out with relief, felt her shudder and twitch beneath him, and then he came hard, rushing into her with a force he hadn't realised was possible.

Pressing himself deep into her, he allowed the pleasure to take him over, holding him suspended in an electric fever that he wanted to go on for ever.

But it didn't. Slowly the feeling subsided and he became aware of Emily crushed beneath him, his still remarkably hard length lying heavy inside her.

Drawing back slowly, he heard her give a deep exhalation of breath and raised his head to look at her, not entirely sure what sort of a reaction he was going to get.

She was beaming at him, her eyes wide and punch-drunk, her mouth red from his rough kisses.

'Well,' she said, pushing herself up to a sitting position. 'That was unexpected.'

'Yeah.'

He ran a hand over his hair, shoving it back out of his eyes and turning away from her to remove the condom and re-dress himself. He swore soundly under his breath, astounded with himself for giving in to his base urges so easily when he'd been doing so well to resist her up until this point.

When he turned back she'd pulled the skirt of her dress down to cover herself again and was eyeing him warily. 'Don't worry—I'm on the pill as well, so there's very little chance of any accidents happening. I always use two types of protection, just in case.'

He shot up an eyebrow. 'You're *that* worried about getting pregnant?'

'I'm not the sort of person who should have kids,' she said flatly.

'Why not?' he asked, frowning.

She shrugged but didn't meet his eye. 'I'm too selfish.'

The false levity in her voice disturbed him. 'That's not how Lula paints you.'

She looked up to meet his gaze, her expression guarded. 'So Lula let slip about my mum not being dead, huh?'

'Yes.'

She sighed. 'Look, I'm sorry I lied, but I didn't think I needed to tell you the truth. You didn't seem very interested in really getting to know me. And I was worried it might have an impact on our deal and possibly ruin our chances of having Lula's wedding here.' She swiped a hand in the air. 'Anyway, it doesn't matter since I'll be completely out of your life in about a week.'

His stomach clenched with disquiet, but he shook it off. He didn't want to think about what it would be like never to see her again right now.

Moving to sit down on the desk next to her, he turned to recapture eye contact. 'What won't matter, Emily? What's going on with your mother?'

Her eyes widened in surprise. 'Lula didn't tell you?'

'No. She wouldn't say any more. She said to ask you,' he said, beginning to worry about what she might be about to tell him—especially after what they'd just done.

She took a breath. 'My mum's in a psychiatric hospital.'

He stared at her in surprise. That wasn't at all what he'd been expecting her to say. 'Why?' he managed to get out eventually.

'She has severe cyclical bipolar disorder. She gets violent and tries to hurt other people. And herself.'

'Why would you feel you had to hide that from me?'

She let out a snort. 'I don't know. Maybe I'm worried you'll think I'm crazy too?'

He blinked. 'Are *you* worried that you are?'

She didn't answer him—just stared down at the floor.

'Surely you'd know by now if you were bipolar?' he asked, feeling a shot of unease at trying to discuss a subject he knew nothing about.

She shrugged. 'I get this feeling bubbling up in me some days—like I'm walking on the edge of something dangerous. It scares me.'

He swiped a hand across his forehead. 'Hell, we all

feel like we're walking a fine line between sanity and madness some days.'

She glanced over and gave him a crooked smile. 'Yeah. I know that. I don't seriously think I have it.'

There was an awkward pause and she slid off the table and smoothed down her dress and hair. 'Anyway, now you know,' she said, with a hint of challenge in her voice.

They stared at each other again. The strange tension was making him jumpy. He had no clue what she must be thinking.

'Look, I should get back to the wedding before Lula wonders where I am,' she said abruptly, making a move towards the door.

'Yes, of course.'

He watched her as she turned the lock to let herself out.

'Listen…' he said, making a quick decision before she could disappear.

As she'd pointed out, they'd only be in each other's lives for another week or two, and it would be stupid not to take advantage of their mutual attraction now they'd jumped over the line. It would just be sex. He felt pretty sure now that she would be okay with that. He certainly was.

'I'm staying in the guesthouse tonight, so one of Lula's guests can use my room. Come over later—after the reception finishes.'

She turned back to face him, her expression curiously blank, not giving him any clues as to how she felt about his suggestion.

'It doesn't matter what time,' he said, keeping his tone nonchalant and breezy. He raised a provocative eyebrow. 'You still owe me two orgasms, remember? Then we're even.'

To his relief she broke into a wide grin. 'Sure. I'll be there.'

He smiled back. 'See you later, Emily.'

As soon as she felt it was late enough that she could excuse herself from the wedding party Emily went in search of Lula, her body humming with excitement at the thought of getting up close and personal with Theo again.

The sex had been amazing—totally unexpected, but all the better for it—and she wanted more of it. Lots more. His constant rejection of her had been something that had tainted everything she'd done recently, and she was relieved at the idea of the world being set back to rights so things could go back to normal.

Finally finding Lula, tipsy and glowing with happiness in Tristan's arms on the makeshift dance floor, she made her excuses, smiling sedately at Lula's hopeful suggestion that she was sneaking off for an illicit rendezvous with Theo.

She wasn't ready to tell her friend about what was going on with him just yet. Mostly because she didn't really know herself.

She was pretty sure this was just going to be a short, hot fling, but something in the back of her brain nagged at her not to totally discount it being more. It wasn't as though she was expecting it to turn into a serious relationship, but the thought of never seeing him again made her stomach twist uncomfortably.

He opened the door of the guesthouse to her wearing a pair of jeans and an old T-shirt—which mercifully didn't her take long to strip off him.

After she'd paid him his orgasms back they lay in bed together, her snuggled into his body as he ran his fingers lazily along her arm from shoulder to elbow.

It felt so good to be allowed to get this close to him finally, and her body began to relax and grow heavy with tiredness as the sun made an appearance through the chinks in the curtains.

'So, are you going to tell me why you've been rejecting my determined advances for so long?' she murmured, intrigued to see whether he'd give something away whilst in this relaxed, dreamlike state.

'No.'

Propping herself onto her elbow, she frowned down at him. 'Why not?' she asked, her frustration coming out clearly in her tone.

His expression remained shuttered. 'Because I don't want to talk about that stuff. Deal with it.'

'Argh! You're *such* a pain in the butt,' she said, forcing as much levity into her voice as she could manage.

He turned to lift a sardonic eyebrow at her. 'Is this your sneaky way to get me riled up and inside you again?'

Flashing him a grin, feeling relieved he hadn't totally shut her out again, she ran a fingertip around his nipple. 'Might be. We clearly have spectacular angry sex.'

'You like a bit of *angry*, don't you?'

She narrowed her eyes. 'It adds to the excitement.'

'It's a good job, since I'm such a surly bastard. Hugo used to tease me mercilessly about it. He was the smart, funny one—and incredibly brave. He knew he wasn't going to be around that long but he never let it get him down. I was always the grumpy one.'

'He sounds amazing.'

'He was. I still miss him.'

'Of course you do—that's only natural.' She dropped her gaze to where her hand played against his chest.

'How long has it been since you saw your mother?' he

asked bluntly, clearly wanting to turn the conversation away from him and back to her.

A cold chill swept through her body at the mention of her. 'I don't know. A long time.'

'Will you ever go and see her?'

She shrugged. 'What's the point? She doesn't want to see me. As my father so unsubtly pointed out, many a time, if she loved me at all she wouldn't have tried to kill herself. Twice.'

He put his hand over hers in shock, then squeezed it in sympathy. 'Jeez, Emily, and I thought *my* mother was hard work.'

'She's a pussycat in comparison to mine. You know, the first time she tried to commit suicide was on my thirteenth birthday. I came home early, excited about the party she was meant to be throwing for me, and found her in the bath with her wrists cut. She'd left a note addressed to my brother, telling him she loved him. I got nothing. Not even a passing mention. She didn't even love me enough to say goodbye. I decided at that point that she may as well be dead, so that's what I tell people.'

His hand tightened on hers. 'You can't blame yourself. Clearly she was having some kind of breakdown.'

She flicked her gaze to meet his. 'It's telling that she chose my birthday as the day she wanted to die, though. I was a bit—challenging when I was younger. I was particularly obnoxious as a tween. I think I drove her mad. Literally.'

She gave a cynical laugh, which he frowned at.

'Although fairly recently a friend of the family let slip that my mum seemed to become very depressed soon after my brother was born and she found out my dad was having an affair,' she continued, lying back down next to him on the bed, suddenly exhausted from all the confessing. 'I guess the combination of all those things together must have tipped her over the edge.'

'It's never just one thing,' he said, sliding an arm under her neck and pulling her into a hug against his body.

'My father wouldn't let me talk about it,' she said to his chest, her voice sounding loud in the ear pressed against him. 'It was as if it hadn't happened. Any time I mentioned it, or got upset, he'd shut me down. He had no idea how to handle it, so he didn't. I think he's bitter about it because he believes she deliberately hid her depression from him before he married her. He feels duped, or something—landed with a defective wife. At least that's how he justifies locking her away.'

'You were very young to have to deal with all that,' he said, his voice rumbling through the wall of his chest.

'Yeah, I guess. After her first attempt my father wouldn't let her see me and my brother and she tried to commit suicide again a couple of months later. That's when he had her committed. Very quietly, of course. He told any friends who asked that she'd left him to go and live with her lover in Italy and didn't want to have contact with any of us again.'

Theo let out a huff of sympathetic disbelief.

'It's amazing how easily people believed she'd just run off with a lover to another country without a word. I guess the friends she had weren't that close to her. Or maybe she'd annoyed them all by flirting with their husbands. According to my father, she was quite the seductress in her day. No wonder he hates the way I live my life. I'm sure he thinks that sex is the essence of pure evil and it's going to be my downfall—even though his own affair probably contributed to my mother's breakdown.'

'Is he single now?'

'*Ha!* No. He found himself a meek and pliant mistress soon after my mother "ran away" and he's gradually moved her into his life. In fact he's never admitted it but I suspect she was the woman he had the affair with before. Anyway, everyone assumes she's his wife and my mother now. I can't stand her.'

'So you haven't seen any of your family for a long time, then?'

She shook her head, walking her fingers up from his belly button to his chest and back down again. 'No. You should see the way my father looks at me, Theo—like he's watching for the warning signs that my mother displayed and is worried I'm going to spontaneously go crazy on him. That's why I never see him any more. I can't stand the look in his eyes. When I was young people used to tell me I was just like my mother all the time. Even down to her mannerisms. No wonder he can't bear to be around me.'

'He's wrong to treat you like that, Emily,' Theo said forcefully.

She lifted her head to look him in the eye and gave him a grateful smile.

'Anyway, it doesn't matter. I'm fine. I have a job I love, good friends and a life I enjoy living.'

She tried not to think about how it could all fall down around her ears soon, if the producers of her show had their way and replaced her with Daisy Dunlop. Rolling on top of him, she kissed him long and deep to take her mind off it.

It would all be fine.

She'd make sure it was.

CHAPTER SEVEN

AFTER BLEARILY WAVING Tristan and Lula off on their honeymoon at midday the next day, Theo and Emily went back to bed and slept till the afternoon, waking to have slow, lazy sex again, then doze in the late afternoon sun that poured in through the large windows of the guesthouse until Emily maintained she really had to go back home to London.

As much as she'd loved finally breaking through Theo's iron control and making up for the time they'd wasted, she didn't want to give him the impression she was moving in to stay. In fact she was confused about exactly what she *did* want from him.

She'd assured him she wasn't a hearts and flowers person, and was not looking for anything serious, but after confessing her deepest, darkest secrets to him the night before their connection felt edgy and a little more unbalanced than she was comfortable with. He'd given no indication at all that he was interested in taking this thing further, and he was still refusing to tell her anything personal about himself, so she needed to be careful here.

So, after she'd finally peeled herself away from his addictive company, she made her way back home.

Her flat felt very small and cramped after being at

Theo's place, and she wasn't able to stay in it long before the urge to go out again took hold of her.

She met up with some friends at a pub in Covent Garden, and flirted a little with some men she met at the bar, but the experience didn't satisfy her as it should have.

She left early, citing tiredness—which her friends ribbed her about—and was glad when she got home and was able to fall into bed. Drifting off into sleep, she told herself that things would be fine between her and Theo because neither of them wanted a proper relationship, so neither of them would have any trouble walking away at the end. After all, there had hardly even been a beginning.

The next morning she woke to an urgent answer machine message from her agent, pointing out that the production company still hadn't sent through her contract to host the new and improved version of *Treasure Trail* on the more highbrow channel it was moving to, and that they were fobbing him off when he chased them about it.

It was time to get serious and sort this thing out once and for all.

Taking a deep breath, she called the executive producer on his personal mobile.

He answered with a terse, 'Yup.'

'Ben, it's Emily. What the hell's going on with my new contract? Apparently my agent hasn't had anything from you, and filming starts in less than a month.'

There was a long pause before he replied, as if he was waving for someone to shut up in the background. 'Ah, yes…about that. There might be some changes being made to the show.'

Her skin goosebumped as a feeling of unease flooded through her. 'What do you mean?'

'Look, Emily, the thing is some of the new station

heads have been bandying around the idea of replacing you with Daisy Dunlop—you know, the ex—'

'I know who she is, Ben,' she snapped, before she could stop herself.

There was an offended pause on the other end of the line.

'I'm sorry for being short with you,' she said quickly, 'but you can't blame me for being worried I'm about to lose my job.'

'I get it, Emily, but hold your nerve, okay? We're meeting soon to finalise everything and I'll let you know as soon as I have all the information. I'll be rooting for you. I want you to stay.'

'Hmm…' She couldn't quite bring herself to believe that. The two of them had always had what she'd describe as a tricky relationship, at best.

'So, what have you been up to since the filming wrapped?' he asked, clearly keen to divert her away from the subject of her potential ousting.

That was okay, though, because it gave her an opportunity to point out that she was capable of non-sensational behaviour. 'I've been helping my best friend with her wedding and hanging out at my boyfriend Theo's place.' She cringed a little at the word *boyfriend*, but told herself that what Theo didn't know about wouldn't hurt him.

'The Earl?'

'Yes.'

He let out a surprised laugh. 'So you're really serious about this guy? I thought it was just another one of your over-the-top publicity stunts.'

Prickly irritation wound through her insides. 'Nope. We're serious. As serious as you can get.' She was damned if she was going to let Ben try and make her feel bad about how she chose to live her life.

'As in *engaged* serious?'

She shifted uneasily on the sofa, but held her nerve. 'Well, I wouldn't like to say, Ben. Especially as our friends and family haven't heard us say that word yet,' she said, loading her voice with innuendo and feeling a sneaking sense of shame at the little white lie. Not that Theo would ever get to hear about it. It was unlikely that his and Ben's paths would ever cross.

'Then I guess congratulations are in order.'

'Why? Are you guaranteeing my continued place on the show?'

He laughed. 'You don't give up, do you?'

'Never.'

'Well, I suppose if you've managed to turn a corner in your personal life that will probably play well with the new station execs. Are you bringing him to that film premiere on Thursday evening? It would probably help if they saw pictures of you there with him.'

She slapped a hand against her forehead. She'd totally forgotten that she needed to arrange a date for that.

She liked to go to as many awards ceremonies and film premieres as possible, to keep her face in the magazines and her profile up in the press, and the production company liked it too because it meant free publicity for the show. Usually she took one of the men she'd had short, no-strings flings with in the past to be arm candy. They accepted her invitations because they knew they'd get exposure out of it too—as well as some hot thank-you sex afterwards—but she didn't want to ask one of them and have it reported that she was seeing someone else while Theo's mother was under the impression the two of them were having a serious relationship.

So that meant only one thing. She was going to have

to persuade Theo to go with her—and, based on his reluctance to be in the public eye, that was going to take some serious negotiating.

Theo had just finished a project in his workshop and was about to go back over to the house when Emily appeared at the door.

'Hey,' he said, walking over, wiping the grease off his hands with a rag.

He'd been a little disturbed to find he'd missed her company in the last couple of days, after the intensity of being with her at the wedding, but he'd put it down to the unexpected breaking of his sexual fast. The stuff she'd told him about her mother had played on his mind too, but he'd tried hard to put it to one side, determined not to allow any emotional involvement to mar their fling. It had been interesting getting an insight into the reasons for her wild behaviour, but he didn't want to dig any deeper. It wasn't any of his business.

'Hey, yourself. I hope you don't mind me dropping in without calling, but I had a free day so I thought I'd come and see whether you fancied a bit of company.' She wiggled her eyebrows in a suggestive manner and his body immediately sprang to life.

He tossed the rag onto the bench next to her. 'I don't mind. Actually, I was just thinking about calling you to arrange that final meet-up with my mother.'

'Okay, well, I guess I came at a good time, then,' she said, stepping closer so she could brush something out of his hair. She gave him a provocative smile. 'You're all dirty.'

He raised an eyebrow. 'I was just about to go and take a shower.'

Her pupils dilated, the black almost swallowing the

gold of her irises, and the corner of her mouth twitched up into a grin. 'I could do with a shower too,' she said, her voice suddenly rough and low.

He didn't need any more encouragement than that.

Without another word, he grabbed her hand and led her out of the workshop and over to the manor house, practically running with her up the stairs to his en-suite bathroom, where he stripped her out of her jeans and T-shirt, tossing his own clothes onto the pile while she went to turn on the shower.

He caught hold of her before she got under the water and kissed her hard and deep, luxuriating in the feel of her soft skin pressed against his, from chest to hip. He was as hard as stone already, and the pressure of his erection between their bodies nearly drove him insane with the need to bury himself inside her.

Stepping back carefully into the shower cubicle, he pulled her with him, feeling the warm water rain down on his back and onto his hair.

Drawing away from him, she looked around for the shower gel, locating it on the shelf behind him, and poured some of it onto her palm. Rubbing it first between her hands, she then lathered it all over him, paying particular attention to the place he could really do without her rubbing too hard right then. Even though it had only been a couple of days his body was reacting as though it had been weeks since he'd last been inside her, and he worried for a moment that he'd come too quickly if she continued to give that much devotion to her task.

Thankfully she seemed to sense his slight withdrawal from her touch and instead pulled the showerhead off its holder and hosed him down with it, sluicing water over his sensitised skin as she washed the soapy bubbles away.

'That's better,' she said, with a wicked smirk on her

face, before kneeling down and taking the tip of his shaft into her mouth, swirling her tongue around the head with such expertise he had to press both hands against the walls of the cubicle to steady himself.

She took him deep, then pulled back, then deep again, and he groaned with the acute pleasure of it, sliding one hand into her hair and gliding his thumb over her cheek.

'Emily, if you want to get some of your own action right now you're going to have to go slow with me,' he muttered.

She laughed with him still inside her mouth and the vibration of it nearly sent him over the edge.

Pulling away from him, she stood up and stepped out of the cubicle, going over to the bathroom cabinet and coming back with a condom clutched between her fingers. Maintaining eye contact, she tore the packet open and rolled it onto the hard length of him, her eyes telling him exactly what sort of pleasure he was about to experience. Putting the flats of her hands against his chest, she guided him to stand with his back against the cubicle wall and turned her back on him, leaning her hands against the glass in front of her and pushing backwards towards him in invitation.

He didn't need more urging than that, and after positioning himself carefully he slid inside her, echoing her gasp of pleasure as their bodies connected.

They moved together, her hands making a squeaking sound on the glass as his thrusts pushed her back and forth.

'Theo?' she gasped as he leant forward and propped one hand on the wall above her head for balance.

'Yeah?' he said, feeling his orgasm begin to build as they moved together.

'I need to ask you a favour.'

'Now?' he groaned, barely able to concentrate on speaking, let alone process a request for his help.

She pushed hard against him, forcing him to stop moving. 'I need a date for a thing on Thursday night. A film premiere. Will you go with me?'

It seemed like a perfectly reasonable request if it meant she would just start bloody *moving* again. 'Yes. Fine. I'll go with you,' he said, the acceptance barely registering in his consciousness as she relaxed her stance and allowed him to thrust hard into her again.

He would have done just about anything for her at that moment.

'You didn't mention the entire phalanx of the British press were going to be at this thing,' Theo muttered into Emily's ear as they walked away from the cab that had dropped them on the edge of Leicester Square and pushed their way through the thronging crowds to the cinema where the film premiere was being held.

'Ah, it's just a few reporters—they won't bite,' she said, attempting to brush his irritation away with her hand.

He stopped walking and folded his arms across his broad chest, giving her an angry frown. 'You knew it was going to be this much of a zoo, didn't you?' he said coldly. 'No wonder you asked me to come while you had me so distracted.'

'I don't think I've ever needed to *ask* you to come,' she teased, straightening his tie with a slightly shaking hand and trying to ignore the sinking feeling of guilt in her stomach.

She knew she hadn't exactly played fair, but he wouldn't have said yes if she'd casually mentioned it over dinner, so she'd had to resort to using the only persuasive device she'd had available. Ordinarily, she wouldn't have even considered it, but this outing could be the difference between her keeping her spot on the show or sinking into obscurity.

Taking a step backwards, she gave him a complimentary up-and-down look. 'You scrub up well, *My Lord*.'

He continued to scowl at her and she flashed him a pleading grin back.

'It's just walking down a bit of red carpet, then watching a film in a cinema that's closed to the public, Theo. What can possibly be so terrible about that?'

He didn't reply, just kept giving her that steely-eyed look of his.

She picked up his hand and squeezed it hard. 'Look, it'll be fine. Just walk next to me and don't answer any questions if we get asked any. Let me handle it. Okay?'

She leaned forward and attempted to kiss the scowl off his face.

'Theo?' she murmured, pressing herself against him.

'Yes. Fine,' he said tersely. 'But I want to make it clear that I'm not happy about this and it will *never* happen again.'

'That much I gathered,' she said, flashing him a wry grin as relief poured through her.

Tugging on his hand, she urged him to follow her towards the cordoned-off area that celebrity guests, cast and crew members had to walk through to join the beginning of the red carpet.

Leicester Square was alive tonight, with the hubbub of excitement coming from fans of the actors in the film as well as the usual throng of tourists that made the square one of the busiest in London.

She loved it.

The buzz of excitement that went with these kinds

of events always thrilled her. She was like a moth to a flame when it came to the bright lights of a public spectacle such as this. She'd always loved the adoration of strangers, not ever having had the adoration of a family to rely on, and she didn't think she'd ever be able to give it up. Luckily her position as host of a show as popular as *Treasure Trail* had kept her in the nation's interest, but she was well aware that fame was a fickle mistress and could turn on her at any moment.

Hopefully that moment wouldn't be for a very long time—if ever.

After showing their invitations to two burly-looking bouncers at the cordon, they were ushered through to the beginning of the plush red carpet synonymous with film and fame.

'Okay—you ready?' she said, giving him a look of what she hoped was persuasive positivity.

'No. But let's do this thing,' he replied, the scowl still evident on his face.

They'd only walked a couple of paces down the almost blindingly brightly lit catwalk when a journalist called out to them to stop and a wave of camera flashes went off in their faces.

She felt Theo's hand tighten in hers and she gave it a reassuring squeeze back and led him over to the journalist who had called out to them, flashing the smile she was so famous for.

'Emily! Marnie White from the *Daily Courier*. So, a little birdy—in the shape of your executive producer—tells me that congratulations are in order?'

Emily gave the woman a blank stare, wondering why Ben had told a journalist about his decision to keep her on at *Treasure Trail* before he'd talked to her about it. Surely that couldn't be right?

'You mean about the show moving to a new channel?' she asked with a stiff smile, hating the idea of being caught out like this in full public view. Even though it sounded as if it was going to be good news about the show she would have preferred to hear it from Ben first, so she could have had more time to formulate an upbeat soundbite for the press.

The journalist nodded towards Theo. 'No, I'm talking about the two of you, tying the knot.'

She felt Theo freeze beside her.

Something hot and heavy dropped into her stomach, sending a wave of nausea up into her throat.

Oh, no.

'So who's invited to the wedding?' the journalist continued, seemingly unaware of the chaos she'd just caused, loading her voice with implication and batting her eyelashes to make sure Emily got the message.

Oh, she'd got the message all right. She was totally and utterly *screwed.*

'Uh…'

She needed to pull herself together. *Fast.*

'You know me, Marnie, I'm a very private person. I don't like to comment on my personal life,' she managed to mumble through frozen lips.

Her heart was beating so hard against her ribs she thought it might explode out of her body at any moment. She almost hoped it would—at least then they'd lead with a story about that instead of her supposed engagement to Theo.

All the journalists listening in, as well as Marnie, burst out laughing at that totally ridiculous statement. And quite fairly so. Never in her life had she shied away from courting the press in order to get publicity.

Deciding the best possible move was to run like the

wind, she shot Marnie a cool smile and walked away quickly, hoping not to look too conspicuous in her hurry, pulling a very tense Theo along with her.

Her false grin was actually making her jaw ache by the time they escaped from the press line and into the cool, comparatively calm lobby of the large cinema.

People were milling about, drinking complimentary wine while they waited to be seated, so she dragged Theo into a quiet corridor leading to the other smaller cinemas, which weren't being used in order to keep the rest of the venue exclusively for the premiere.

'What the *hell* was that?' Theo hissed, as soon as they were out of earshot of any of the other patrons.

His eyes flashed with anger as she gave him a horrified smile.

'I'm so sorry. I had no idea that was going to happen.'

He threw up his hands in disgust. 'Don't you have *any* integrity? You *really* think it's okay to lie about the status of our relationship to the press to get more exposure for your career?'

She held out both hands to him, begging for his understanding. 'They're talking about taking my show away from me, Theo. I can't let them do that. I thought if they saw me supposedly settling down they'd think I was a better fit for the tone they want to project with the show now.'

'So you thought you'd lie about being engaged to an *earl*?'

His voice was so icy it made a shiver run down her spine.

'It wasn't—' She took a deep steadying breath. 'I never meant it to come out publicly. My exec producer misheard something I said and just assumed we were engaged. I didn't correct him. I didn't think it would cause this much trouble.'

He folded his arms across his chest. 'Perhaps you were hoping that once the news got out I'd have trouble backing out of it in case my mother found out?'

Her jaw dropped in outrage. 'What are you saying? That you think I *want* to be engaged to you?'

'Do you?'

'No! I told you—I'm not interested in getting married. I like being single.'

He frowned, his expression flicking between confusion and anger, clearly having trouble believing her.

Her phone chose that moment to beep loudly and announce the arrival of a text message.

'You'd better check that in case it's someone congratulating you on hooking an earl for a husband,' he said coldly, taking a step away from her and leaning against the wall behind them, his arms crossed defensively in front of him.

'Funny,' she muttered, fumbling in her bag to find her phone.

It was a relief to be given an excuse to look away from Theo's angry gaze, and hopefully the distraction would give her a precious few seconds to figure out how to deal with this new, disastrous situation.

Flicking on the screen, she opened up the text.

It was from her brother.

She'd been ducking his calls and deleting his messages without listening to them for the last couple of days, assuming he was going through the motions of his yearly attempt to reconnect with her even though she'd made it perfectly clear she didn't want to have anything to do with him any more.

They'd never got on as children. He was their father's golden child and he'd never let her forget it.

'This really isn't a good time for a family reunion, Jake,' she muttered under her breath, flicking her gaze down the text.

It wasn't a request for a reunion.

Blood pounded through her head as she re-read the words on the screen, thinking she must have misinterpreted them.

After her third time of reading it the message finally sank in, and she let out a long, shaky breath, all the air rushing painfully out of her lungs.

'Emily? What's wrong?' Theo asked, his voice sounding muffled through the fog of her confusion.

'It's my mother,' she whispered, barely able to get the words past her lips. 'She's dead.'

CHAPTER EIGHT

THEO STARED AT Emily in shock as she took a couple of shaky steps backwards, finding the wall with her hands so she could lean on it, the phone slipping through her trembling fingers and bouncing onto the carpet beside her. All the blood seemed to have drained from her face and her eyes looked glassy under the muted light in the cinema corridor.

'Emily?' He made a move towards her, but pulled himself back from touching her at the last second.

He didn't know what to do. He felt he should attempt to comfort her somehow, but he had no idea how to go about it. Dealing with this kind of emotion really wasn't his thing.

'How?' he asked instead, mentally kicking himself at how flippant the question sounded.

Emily didn't seem to notice or care, though, judging by the blank look on her face. 'A blood clot. There's been an enquiry,' she replied, her tone emotionless and flat.

She bent down and scooped her phone up off the floor, her grip so strong it turned her knuckles white. 'The funeral's tomorrow in Guildford,' she whispered, her voice catching on the last word.

Theo's heart went out to her. She suddenly looked so vulnerable and lost—certainly nothing like the peacock-proud Emily he'd known for the last few weeks. He felt an overwhelming urge to draw her into a tight hug against his body, to soothe her, but he knew that would be a mistake. He couldn't possibly give her what she needed.

'Are you going to go?' he asked quietly.

She shook her head. 'I don't think so.'

'You should,' he said, before he could stop himself.

It really wasn't his business, but he had experience with funerals and grief, and if he could offer any advice it would be to go through it now so she could put her mother to rest in her mind and not let it ruin her life later, in a slower, more painful way.

'It could help, Emily—to get you some sort of closure.'

She stared at the floor for one long minute before nodding. 'I guess I should say goodbye…even though she never extended the same courtesy to me.' She drew in a sharp breath, almost like a hiccough of grief.

'Are you okay?' Theo asked, reflexively putting his hand on her arm and feeling her tremble under his touch.

She nodded, then shook her head, clearly unable to speak.

'Let me take you home,' he said, sliding his arm around her shoulders for support and gently propelling her forward towards the exit.

And then, as if she hadn't already had enough bad luck, Marnie from the *Daily Courier* chose that exact moment to appear at the top of the corridor and give them both a curious look as she passed them on her way to the restrooms.

'Everything all right, Emily? You look like you've seen a ghost,' she said, her beady eyes sweeping over the two of them.

'She's fine,' Theo replied tersely, guiding Emily away, towards a quiet side exit, his arm still wrapped tightly around her.

* * *

Emily felt numb. And curiously empty.

Out in the neon-lit night, Theo walked her round to one of the quieter roads and managed to hail a cab while she stood staring sightlessly at the pavement.

Her mother was dead.

And not just in her messed-up imagination any more. She was really gone this time.

She let him manhandle her into the taxi, grateful that someone else was making the necessary decisions, taking control of the everyday motions that she felt strangely unable to handle right at that moment.

After a little gentle coaxing from Theo she mumbled her address to the driver and sat back stiffly in the springy seat next to him as they drove slowly through the busy streets of central London.

Twenty silent and hollow minutes later they reached her house in Notting Hill and she got out on shaking legs, walking swiftly towards her front door while Theo paid for the cab.

He joined her just as she'd managed to get the key into the lock on her third try. It was almost like being drunk, this feeling of floating outside herself, unable to make her limbs and brain function properly together.

Walking into her home, she was only aware that he'd followed her when she heard him close the door behind him and cough gently.

She whipped around, her hands raised as a barrier against him. Now she was in the safety and familiarity of her own place she just wanted to be left alone to process everything.

'You don't need to stay with me. I'm fine.' She turned away from him, heading straight for her bedroom.

'Are you?' he asked, following her.

As she reached the door he caught up with her and spun her round to face him. His brows were drawn down and his eyes radiated concern.

She didn't want his sympathy. Didn't need it. She could do this on her own. Or with her best friend's help.

'Yes. Anyway, I'll call Lula if I need someone.'

'On her honeymoon?'

His point made her freeze in shock. He was right. She'd forgotten that Lula was away. There was no way she could interrupt her friend's honeymoon with news like this. Lula would feel as guilty as hell about not being there for her and it would ruin her holiday.

She knew she could always rely on her friend to be a shoulder to cry on, but Lula had Tristan now and he should be her top priority. Before Lula had got married she'd always had her friend there, rooting for her. Supporting her. Loving her. But now, she realised with a sick, sinking feeling, there was a great gaping hole in her life that she had no idea how to fill.

She was going to have to deal with this alone until Lula came back.

The thought of it made her cold with fear.

She had other friends she could call, of course, but no one she was emotionally close to. She kept most of her relationships light and frivolous, preferring to have lots of easy, non-demanding acquaintances. Plus, none of them even knew her mother had been alive. She'd told them all she was dead, and she didn't want to have to go through the humiliation of having to explain her painful past to someone else right now.

Apart from Lula, Theo was the only other person who knew the truth of the situation—but having him seeing her break into little pieces wasn't something she was prepared to let happen. He'd probably run a mile if she broke down on him now. And who could blame him? Dealing with this kind of thing had never been part of their deal.

'I'm fine, Theo, you don't need to stay,' she muttered, walking into her bedroom, praying he would get the message and turn around and leave.

But instead he followed her into her bedroom.

'Why are you still here? I told you I'm okay,' she said with her back still to him, lacing her voice with irritation in an attempt to repel him.

'Because you need someone to look out for you right now. Someone who's willing and able to put up with your nonsense and know it for what it really is.'

She snorted with disdain and turned to look at him, her heart thumping in her chest. 'And that is…?'

He took a deep breath, fixed her with his dark gaze and took a careful step forward. 'Fear, and an unhealthy proclivity for self-loathing.'

Hot anger flashed through her and she shot him a look of disgust. 'I don't *hate* myself.'

He didn't say anything, just kept looking at her with an infuriatingly shrewd expression.

'I *don't*, Theo.'

He still didn't say anything.

His knowing silence was the last straw.

'Who do you think you are, coming in here and saying things like that to me?' she spat. 'You don't *know* me. Sure, we've had sex and some fun over the last few weeks, but that doesn't mean you've got into my head, Theo.' She was shaking now, her whole body tense with rage.

'I know you, Emily,' he said calmly.

She lost it, flying forward and swiping a hand at him, aiming to slap that supercilious look right off his face. 'You *don't*!'

He blocked her attack, and the next one, putting his arms out in front of him, allowing her blows to rain down on him until she ran out of steam and he was able to grab both her hands and hold her steady.

'Get off me!' she shouted in his face, her breath rasping painfully in her throat.

He shook his head, his brow furrowed.

His silent refusal enraged her even more. 'Get out of my house! I don't want you here. You're not welcome!' she yelled.

He took it, resolutely refusing to rise to her jibes.

He wasn't giving her anything back—just shutting her out like he always did.

She wanted to hurt him—needed to see the same pain she was feeling reflected back at her in his eyes.

'Why so quiet, Theo? Afraid to stand up to me? Just like you're afraid to stand up to your own mother? You'd rather lie and sneak around behind her back than talk to her straight and tell her how you feel. Because you're a *coward*!'

Her caustic words finally seemed to penetrate through his emotional defences and the expression in his eyes grew hard with anger. But to her frustration he still refused to say anything back to her, instead clenching his jaw, making a muscle tick in his cheek.

Desperation clawed at her. She needed a reaction from him. *Any* reaction. Just to prove she'd made some kind of impact on his consciousness. That perhaps he cared about her more than he let on.

Because she cared about *him*.

The realisation hit her like a punch to the chest, knocking the breath out of her lungs.

'Say something, Theo,' she begged, her voice now

wobbly with the emotion she was frantically trying to hold back.

He opened his mouth, his dark gaze boring into hers, and for one precious second she thought he might speak. But then he shut his mouth again and released her hands from his grip, his expression detached and unyielding. He gave her one last cold look before turning and walking away.

She listened to his footsteps thundering down the stairs, then the swish and slam of the front door as he left the house, and her heart sank deep into her gut.

He was gone.

He'd deserted her—just like all the other men in her life. Not that she hadn't pushed him to it, but he clearly didn't care about her enough to fight back.

Slumping onto her bed, she put her head in her hands and took some deep, controlling breaths to stop herself from hyperventilating, feeling more alone than she'd ever felt in her life.

She had no idea how she was going to get through tomorrow without his comforting strength by her side.

And the thought of having to deal with her father's cold contempt on top of everything else made her gut sink with misery.

Taking a deep, bolstering breath, she smoothed her shaking hands down her hair and mentally pulled herself together.

She was just going to have to do what she always did. Put a brave face on it.

Theo walked around the streets for an hour after leaving Emily's house, finding cold comfort in his solitude and focusing on the heavy slap of his feet against the pavement to try and keep his mind off what she'd said to him.

After his anger had finally faded to a dull glow in his stomach he allowed himself to turn it over in his mind. She was right, of course. He'd known it deep down in his gut as soon as the words had left her lips.

He was a coward.

He shouldn't have let his mother railroad him the way she had. It was actually pathetic, how he'd resorted to lying to her to get her off his back instead of having an honest, frank conversation and sorting things out once and for all.

But honest conversations had never been his thing. Nor had dealing with the dark swirl of feelings he'd been battling for years now. His foray into the futile world of losing himself in willing bodies had plugged the gap for a while, but once he'd realised it could only be a temporary measure he'd pulled himself out of it—only to be left feeling exposed and lonely. So he'd hidden away from the world. But he still wasn't free. Not until he faced up to what it was that kept him so emotionally aloof from everyone in his life.

He'd accused Emily of being afraid and not loving herself, but he was just as guilty of that as she was.

More, probably—because at least she threw herself into new experiences. He hid. Like the coward he was.

He stopped outside a quiet-looking bar on the street, realising it was late and the city was winding down. It would be so easy to step in there and find solace in the bottom of a bottle of whisky, like he'd used to, maybe even pick up a willing bed partner. But he knew he wasn't going to do that. He couldn't live with the shame of giving in to that again—not when Emily was being so brave.

Deciding it was too late to try and get home, he walked to the nearest hotel and booked himself into it for the night.

Slumping fully clothed onto the bed, he let the memories of the last few weeks play around his head, ending with the last few minutes he'd spent in Emily's company.

He couldn't stop thinking about how wild her eyes had looked when he'd held her away from him, and then how hurt when he wouldn't react to her after her tirade against him.

He rubbed a hand over his face in frustration. He should stop being such a wuss, shying away from anything vaguely resembling strong emotion, and *do something*—something helpful.

He wondered whether she was asleep right now.

He doubted it.

The thought of her driving herself to Guildford in the morning made his gut clench with worry. There was no way he could let her do that—it would be negligent of him as a fellow human being.

She probably wouldn't want him there, but he couldn't in all conscience leave her to deal with the funeral and her hostile family on her own in case they broke through her bubble of protective denial and she found herself having to deal with some truly horrendous feelings alone.

He knew how it went. He'd been through it himself twice already—once with Hugo, then again a few years ago when his father had passed away.

With that decided, he closed his eyes and finally allowed himself to drift off to sleep, feeling more positive and self-assured than he had in a very long time.

After waking early Theo took a shower, then re-dressed in the dark suit and tie he'd been wearing last night for the film premiere, the kismet of it giving him a small zing of satisfaction.

This was right. It was meant to happen.

She answered the door to him wrapped in a towel, her hair wet and hanging loose round her shoulders.

'What are you doing here, Theo?' she whispered, a mixture of shock, wariness and what looked suspiciously like hope flickering in her eyes.

He rubbed a hand through his hair. 'I've come to drive you to the funeral. I can stick around all day today. I don't have anything at home that needs my attention,' he said, refraining from adding *as much as you do* to the end of the sentence.

She must have felt the implication, though, because she gave him a scathing look and wrapped her arms around her middle. 'You don't need to do that, Theo. It was never part of our deal. You don't need to play the role of comforter. We're not in a proper relationship, *remember*?'

He sighed. This was going to be tough. She'd make sure it was. 'I know I don't *need* to. I want to. And so what if we're not in a traditional relationship? I'm not going to just walk away and leave you to deal with this on your own.'

She batted away his concern. 'You should. This has nothing to do with you. No good can come of you sticking your nose into the mess of my family's affairs.'

'Don't be so damned obtuse, Emily. *I'll* decide what is and isn't good for me. I'm coming with you to the funeral,' he said, putting up a rebutting hand before she could object. 'This isn't open for discussion. I'll drive you there and stand near the back, so you can find me if you need me or ignore me if you don't.'

She was staring at him with wide eyes. 'You'd do that for me?'

'Yes.'

'Even after what I said to you last night?'

'Yes.' He didn't look away, just kept his eyes locked with hers.

After a moment her gaze dropped to the floor and her shoulders drooped. 'I'm sorry.'

'Don't be. You were right. But we don't need to dwell on that right now. You have more important things to deal with. We'll talk later.'

Dragging her gaze up, she raised an eyebrow. 'Really? You mean you'll actually *talk* to me?'

He almost reacted with a sharp retort until he saw the teasing in her eyes. Leaning on the doorframe, he gave her a pointed look. 'Only if you let me in.'

After staring at him for a long moment, she finally gave him a curt nod of acceptance. 'Okay. You can drive me. I'd probably be a danger on the roads today anyway.' She took a step back so he could walk inside. 'I'm going to get ready. Help yourself to some coffee if you want it,' she said, gesturing towards what he assumed was the kitchen.

Swivelling on the spot, she disappeared up the stairs and he heard her shut the bedroom door behind her with a slam.

Going into the kitchen-diner, he poured himself a coffee and leaned against the counter while he drank it. The room was done out simply, with tasteful furnishings and just a little pizazz—like the purple velvet chaise longue that she had pushed up under the window. It was Emily all over.

Some alien feeling made him drag a tight breath into his lungs but he shoved it away, refusing to let anything get to him today. She needed him strong and steady, and he wasn't about to let any chinks in his armour make him vulnerable.

She emerged from her bedroom ten minutes later in

a tight black dress which showcased her amazing cleavage and curves. Clearly it was in defiance of her father—she'd mentioned he wasn't exactly a fan of her overtly sexual image.

He attempted to keep his incongruous bodily reaction to the sight of her looking so incredibly sexy hidden by holding the magazine he'd been reading in front of his crotch, but she wasn't fooled. Pulling the supplement out of his hands, she stared down at the tent in his trousers with a raised eyebrow.

'Do we need to take care of that before we go?' she asked, with a lilt of amusement in her voice.

He stared at her, shocked by how breezy she was being, how unaffected—until he realised that the hand she was holding the magazine with was shaking. Clearly she was using the distraction of sex and humour to mask her real feelings.

As usual.

'I'll be fine,' he said, reaching out and pulling her in for a hug.

After a moment's resistance she sank into his arms and allowed him to rock her gently.

'You'll be fine too,' he whispered into her hair, praying he was right and that the funeral wouldn't be the trial of fire he was afraid it might turn into.

Grabbing her car keys, she led him out of the house to where her tiny car was parked and he folded his long legs awkwardly into the driving seat.

'This car was definitely *not* designed for men of my height,' he grumbled, pulling the seatbelt across his body and snapping it into the buckle.

She snorted and smiled at him. 'Oh, I don't know… I think you look cute all bunched up in my little car.'

He let out a snort of derision. 'Cute, indeed.'

Her laughter rang in the tiny space as he pulled out into the heavy London traffic.

It took them an hour to drive just south of Guildford, where she told him she'd grown up badly, and where her father still lived with his partner Betty.

They managed to find a parking space easily at the cemetery, and he pulled on the handbrake and killed the engine before turning to check on her.

Her face looked pale in the late-morning sunshine.

'How are you holding up?' he asked gently.

'Fine. I'm fine.' She nodded, as if trying to convince herself of the fact.

'Are you ready?'

She turned to face him with a look of defiance on her face. 'As I'll ever be.'

He went to open his door and get out, but stopped when she put a hand on his arm.

'Theo? I just wanted to say sorry in advance for anything you might see or hear today. Seriously, knowing my family, anything could happen.'

An image of someone flinging themselves on top of her mother's coffin before it was lowered into the ground flashed into his head, but he dismissed it quickly. He didn't think that was what she meant. Based on what she'd told him about her family already, he wasn't expecting it to be a fond, emotional get-together.

'Don't worry about me; I can handle anything that's thrown my way today. Just concentrate on getting yourself through it. As I said, I'll stand near the back, if you like, so I don't encroach on anything.'

She frowned and flapped a hand at him. 'Don't be ridiculous. You stand next to me. I'm not letting anyone tell me who I can and can't bring with me to my own mother's funeral.'

He knew she was referring to her father, but didn't feel he needed to voice it.

They walked together, hand in hand, to where a small group had already gathered around a coffin in the middle of the graveyard. He felt Emily's grip tighten as they got closer and noticed a tall, handsome man and an older, shorter man, whom he assumed were her brother and father, standing talking together.

Out of the corner of his eye he saw Emily throw back her shoulders and felt her pull him forward as she increased her stride towards them. They stopped just in front of the small group, and they didn't need to wait long before both men turned to look at them—her brother apparently surprised and pleased to see her, her father not so much.

'Emily,' the older man said coolly, affording her only a slight inclination of his head.

'Dad, Jake—this is Theo,' she said, turning to look up at him and give him a smile, which he returned.

He held out his hand to her father, wondering whether the man would have the guts to refuse it.

He didn't.

They shook hands quickly, but firmly, and he turned to shake hands with her brother Jake too.

Just then a middle-aged, petite woman with dark hair cut into a neat bob hurried up to them. 'Michael, the vicar would like a word with you before we begin,' she said.

Emily's father gave her a sharp nod and turned and walked off without bothering to excuse himself.

'Still as charming as ever, I see,' Emily muttered.

'He's finding it all a bit hard to deal with,' the woman with the bob said.

Emily turned on her. 'Really, Betty? I'm sure it must be just *awful* for him to have to finally admit he had a mad wife he locked away for years whilst all the time pretending he was actually married to *you*.'

The woman's face turned pillarbox-red. 'Yes, well…I'd better go and see if they need me too,' she mumbled, and scurried off in the direction that Emily's father had gone.

'That was a bit harsh, Em,' Jake said, folding his arms against his chest.

'You think? I don't think so,' Emily replied, crossing her own arms and staring him out.

Before there was a chance for either of them to say anything further the vicar leading the ceremony called them over and they all shuffled into position in front of the coffin.

Theo held her hand all through the short ceremony, feeling her swaying gently beside him as she stared resolutely in front of her, clearly determined not to cry. He admired her fortitude; he'd cried like a baby at Hugo's funeral, and had even shed a tear at his father's—even though they hadn't been as close as they once were.

When it was finally over, and the coffin had been lowered into the ground, the small party started to drift away. Emily turned and pulled on Theo's hand, as if to ask him to leave quickly with her.

'Don't you want to say goodbye to your brother?' he asked, knowing she'd need a bit of a push to get past that iron-clad pride of hers.

'I don't have anything to say to him,' she said stiffly.

He stopped short and tightened his grip on her hand, urging her to a standstill. 'Emily, I know this isn't any of my business, but if I were you I'd want to at least reconnect with my brother and see whether there was any chance of making things right. I know what it feels like to be cut off from family and, honestly, if I had the chance to make things right with a brother I wouldn't hesitate. None of this was his fault either, and judging by the look on his face when he first saw you I suspect it would mean a lot to him if you at least gave him the opportunity to say his piece. He's probably hurting too.'

She stared at him for one long moment, a whole range of emotions flitting over her face until she finally alighted on resignation. 'Okay. Fine. I'll talk to him—but that's all.'

'Good.' He nodded, surprised but pleased that he'd been able to get through to her. It wasn't like him to get involved in someone else's affairs, but he knew if he didn't at least make her stop and think about how to make things easier on herself no one else would. 'I'll wait for you in the car,' he said, brushing a stray piece of hair away from her face and giving her an encouraging nod.

'Okay. I won't be long,' she said, turning and walking away, towards where her brother was standing talking with the bobbed-haired Betty.

As he walked back to the car a movement in the distance caught his eye and he saw what he thought looked like a flash of sunlight on a camera lens.

Who'd want to take photos in a graveyard? he wondered idly to himself, opening up her car and shoe-horning himself back into it.

Emily walked over to where her brother stood with Betty, her legs shaking less now that the ordeal of the ceremony was over. She'd been terrified of breaking down in front of everyone, and it had only been Theo's robust presence next to her that had kept her strong. He'd been amazing today—truly amazing.

Her insides did a strange little jump at the thought of it.

Jake looked round as she approached, with a surprised but pleased smile on his face.

'Emily—I thought I saw you leaving?'

'I came back.'

He nodded. 'Listen, I'm sorry, but Dad had to get back home quickly for something. He said to say goodbye,' he said, glancing over his shoulder.

She gave a sarcastic laugh. 'No, he didn't, Jake. Why the hell are you covering for him?'

He looked uncomfortable. 'Because I don't think he's right to treat you the way he does.'

'Well, that's big of you—considering you've always been Dad's protégé.'

Jake sighed and ran a hand over his jaw. 'Look, I just wanted to say that I know things were tough when we were young, and I realise that as the oldest you caught the brunt of it all. I was the protected, coddled younger one, and I acted as though you were part of the problem, but I was wrong to do that. I'm really glad you came here today because I wanted the opportunity to say sorry.'

She stared at her brother, sadness rising from deep within her. They'd both been victims, and so young when their world had crashed down around their ears. It was no wonder they'd reacted so badly to it all.

'Apology accepted. And I'm sorry too, for being so impatient with you. It just felt like Dad was always on your side and I didn't handle that well.'

He frowned and went to deny it, but she batted his objection away.

'You always were Dad's favourite. I reminded him too much of Mum, and no matter what I did, or how hard I tried to be who he wanted me to be, he never loved me like he loves you.'

Jake gave her a supportive but sad smile. 'He's not an easy man to please. It's not your fault, Emily.'

'Yeah, that's what I keep telling myself.'

Jake rubbed a hand over his brow. 'Look, I understand why you don't want anything to do with Dad—he's never handled things well—but please don't cut yourself off from me for ever too. I want to get to know you again, Em. Please give me a chance to.'

She sighed and scuffed her toe against the grass. 'I know it's been a long time since we last spoke properly, and that's mostly down to my stubbornness.' She folded her arms across her chest. 'Maybe it's time to put the past behind us.'

'I'd like that.'

She nodded. 'Okay. Although this isn't exactly a great place for a family reunion, is it?' she said, looking round at the emptying graveyard. 'I'll call soon. When I've got my head straight.'

'Okay. Thank you.'

She went to turn away, but then stopped and turned back. 'I wish I'd gone to visit her, Jake. I should have. She was all alone in there. I only ever thought of myself.'

She turned and started to walk away before the painful pressure in her throat gave her away.

Coming here today, she'd finally realised that the slow, dark dread that she'd carried around deep within her, seemingly for ever, was the result of all the guilt and self-loathing that had plagued her since her mother's first suicide attempt.

Theo had been right. She had hated herself. Or if not hated, then she hadn't liked herself very much. And she'd never been brave enough to face her mother or her past so she'd hidden from it. *She* was the coward.

Urgh, she was so messed up.

'She wasn't alone,' Jake said behind her.

She froze and swivelled back to face him. 'What do you mean?'

He gestured to the woman still standing next to him. She'd been so quiet and still that Emily had forgotten she was there. 'Betty used to visit her once a month, without Dad knowing. She told me the day Mum died. She wanted me to know she hadn't been totally on her own in there.'

She turned to face Betty now, her heart pounding in her throat. 'Is that true?'

The woman nodded solemnly.

'Why?' The question came out as a whisper.

'Because your father was never going to do it and I couldn't let her be totally alone.'

'Wow.' She stared at the woman and felt heat rush up her neck into her face. 'Well, that's very kind of you, Betty. It's more than I ever did.'

Betty put her hand on Emily's arm and patted it awkwardly before retracting it again. 'You mustn't blame yourself, Emily. She didn't know who or where she was a lot of the time. She was a very sick woman.'

'But I never visited her.' The raw truth made something in her chest squeeze painfully hard.

'She knew why that was,' Betty said, giving her a supportive smile. 'She'd done the most selfish, cruel thing in the world to you by trying to end her life and then having you find her in that state when you were just a child. She never forgave herself for that. But she loved you. She always loved you. During her lucid times she followed your career religiously...watched your show. She was proud of what you'd achieved with your life and she told me that repeatedly. She was sad that you didn't want to visit her, but she refused to let me come and talk to you. She said you'd been through enough without her badgering you to forgive her, and that she knew you must love her if you were still angry with her. She made me promise not to say anything.'

Betty looked sheepish now, as if she thought she'd done the wrong thing by keeping this information secret until now.

Emily gave her a grateful smile, wanting her to know she didn't blame her. It hadn't been her responsibility. As Theo had pointed out, it hadn't been any one person's fault. They'd all had a hand in it.

'Thank you for visiting her, Betty. I really appreciate you doing that. It was kind of you—especially when she wasn't really anything to do with you.'

'It was my pleasure.'

Betty nodded and turned to walk away, but Emily put her hand on her shoulder to stop her.

'I misjudged you, Betty. I'm sorry I did that.'

Betty gave her a genuinely warm smile back. 'It's okay, Emily. I understand why.'

Walking back to the car to meet Theo, she ran through everything she'd just been told. She felt barely able to process all that had happened as it swirled around her mind like some kind of dizzying zoetrope of pictures.

Her mother had loved her. And even though she'd been very sick she'd known that Emily loved her too, deep down. She felt sure that was true.

Thanks to Betty she hadn't been totally on her own for all those years, and had even gone so far as to follow her career.

The thought of it nearly blew her mind. She wondered how she would have felt during filming if she'd known her mother would be watching the show. Pretty compromised, she suspected. In some ways not knowing had allowed her to truly be herself, without fear of offending, alienating, or even worse trying to please the people she loved.

Because she *did* love them. All of them. Even her father. She just hadn't wanted to admit it for fear of it breaking her.

She found Theo crammed into her little car, listening to the radio with the seat raked back so he could relax into it. He readjusted the seat and flicked off the programme he was listening to when she got into the car with him.

'How did it go?' he asked, one eyebrow raised in suspense.

'Good. It was good. I think it's going to be okay with Jake. I told him I need some time to process everything, then I'll be back in touch.'

Theo nodded. 'That's great, Emily. I'm really pleased to hear it.'

She flashed him a grin. 'Thanks for coming with me. It was good to have you here.'

He didn't say anything—just gave her an understanding smile.

There was a strange moment of tension when neither of them spoke and the question of what happened next hung heavily in the air between them.

'So, what are you up to for the rest of the day?' she asked, trying to sound as casual as possible whilst also steeling herself for being told he had to get back home and had lots to do.

She so desperately didn't want to lose his company now. She had so much to tell him.

Eventually.

When she got it all straight in her own head.

She was acutely aware that if it hadn't been for him she never would have spoken to Jake or found out about her mother from Betty.

Not that she had any right to drag him further into this. He'd already gone above and beyond the call of duty, coming here with her today. She needed to remind herself that he wasn't her boyfriend. He wasn't even a friend—not really—and he wasn't interested in a relationship with her. He'd made that very plain.

Many times.

'No plans,' he said, his gaze still fixed on hers. 'I'd like it if you came back to my place and had something to eat.'

His voice sounded just as casual as hers had, but she felt the sincerity of his statement and an acute sense of relief rushed through her. Even if he was only interested in sex she'd be happy to lose herself in that with him today.

Wouldn't she?

Yes.

She could do that.

Ignoring a low pull of uneasiness, she smiled and nodded. 'Okay, that would be great. I don't have any food at my house anyway.'

'Good.' He nodded, as if he hadn't been in any doubt that she'd agree.

'Then drive us home, chauffeur,' she said, forcing her mouth into a cheeky grin.

He snorted. 'And *I'm* supposed to be the entitled one,' he said, turning on the ignition and ramming the gearstick into reverse.

Emily was quiet all the way back to his house—via her house so she could pick up a fresh outfit. There was a heavy weariness about her that he'd never seen before and it bothered him. She hadn't shown much emotion throughout the funeral. The only sign that it had affected her at all was the way she'd gripped his hand harder as her mother's coffin had been lowered into the ground.

She hadn't shed a single tear in his company since she'd heard the news about her mother's death.

Clearly it still hadn't fully sunk in yet, and she was riding the denial with her usual brash aplomb.

Not that he was going to push her to talk. She'd get to it when she was ready. He felt sure of that.

Back at his house, they both took a shower and changed into more comfortable clothes before reconvening in the kitchen.

After eating a light tea provided by his housekeeper, they moved into the drawing-room to read books and listen to music in the late-afternoon sunshine.

Despite his promise to himself not to get tangled up in the emotion of the situation he couldn't help but keep looking over to make sure she wasn't too exhausted, faking her strength after the excesses of the day. After the fourth time he did this she sighed and put her book down.

'You can stop checking to see whether I'm about to burst into tears on you,' she said crossly.

He snorted. 'Okay,' he said, holding up his hands in surrender. 'Whatever you say.'

She bristled. 'I can take care of myself, you know.'

'I know that, Emily. I just don't want you to feel like you have to today.'

She frowned. 'What? You're going to adopt me now? Take me under that big protective wing of yours?'

Her voice was jokey, but he sensed an undercurrent of seriousness.

'Only if you need me to.' He didn't want to brush her off in case she was angling to talk, but he knew this was a fine line he was treading. She was independent through and through, and wouldn't respond well to any attempt to force a confrontation she didn't want to have.

'I don't *need* you, Theo,' she scoffed, keeping her tone light, but he could tell she was holding back. She was a tigress and there was no way she'd ever be tamed. Not that he wanted to do that. He loved her just as she was.

The realisation struck him hard, forcing the breath right out of his lungs.

He was *in love* with her.

She was staring at him, waiting for his pithy reply, but he had nothing. He was literally speechless.

Clearly she thought he wasn't saying anything back because he didn't agree with her statement and she got up, her body suddenly stiff with anger, colour flooding her cheeks.

'I didn't come here looking for sympathy, Theo.'

He stood up too, frowning hard, totally unsure about how to handle the situation now. He was reeling from the insight about how he really felt about her. How he'd felt for a while now.

Her gaze bored into his and he felt more exposed than he had in a very long time. Frighteningly so. He couldn't speak. Couldn't formulate a plan. So he just stood there, frowning and being ineffectual.

'I think I should go,' she said curtly, brushing her hair away from her face with a shaking hand and walking past him towards the door.

He caught her arm as she passed and swung her back to face him, not sure what to say, but knowing he had to say *something* before she walked away from him for good.

'Don't, Emily. Stay.'

She tried to shrug off his grip but he held her fast. 'You can't make me, Theo.'

'I know that, but I think you should.'

'Why?'

He shook his head. He wanted to have the courage to say it. To tell her how he really felt. But the words wouldn't come. They were jammed painfully in his throat.

'You don't really want me here, Theo. You just feel like you have to play the big man, to save the damsel in distress.'

He shook his head again, but it only seemed to enrage her more.

'Let go of me, Theo. I need to get out of here.'

Her voice sounded panicky now, and she pulled away from him again hard—but he clung on.

'No. I'm not letting you go.'

She stared at him wildly for a few seconds, her eyes filled with the hurt he'd sensed hiding inside her all day, and then her face crumpled, fat tears welling in her eyes before spilling down her cheeks in a torrent. Her brows drew together and she dropped her head, seemingly unwilling for him to witness her pain.

Releasing his grip on her arm, he wrapped his arms around her and held her tightly; stroking his hands down her back and making soothing noises into her hair.

She sobbed in his arms, her whole body shaking with the ferocity of her grief, and still he clung on, absorbing the throbs and shivers of her torment. He wanted to take her pain away, take it himself and hold onto it for her until she'd worked out how to deal with it, but he knew he couldn't do that. All he could do was be there while she accepted it and fought through it herself.

After a few minutes she seemed to get her convulsions under control and he relaxed his hold slightly, intending to lean back and look her in the eyes, to let her know with his expression that it was okay to do this—that he was here for her.

'Don't let go,' she whispered. 'Please don't let go.'

So he pulled her in tight again and they rocked gently together, her breathing growing slower as she began to get it under control.

After another minute of clinging to him she finally relaxed her hold and moved away a little. He released her and took a step back so he could look at her.

'Can I get you anything?' he asked, running his thumbs over her cheeks to brush away her tears.

She gave him a watery smile. 'Some tissues wouldn't go amiss.'

He nodded and left her standing there, with her arms wrapped around herself, while he fetched her some.

She accepted them with a grateful smile and dabbed at her face, then blew her nose, keeping her gaze averted from his. 'I must look a real mess,' she said, her voice laced with self-disgust.

'You look beautiful. You always look beautiful,' he said sincerely, stroking a hand down her arm.

Looking up at him, she gave him a teasing grin. 'You old smoothie, you.'

The switch to levity made him feel first relieved, then inexplicably sad. She was such a strong person—much stronger than him.

'What can I do to help?' he asked, praying she wouldn't say *Let me go home*.

'Come to bed with me?' she asked, her voice a little more wary now, as if she couldn't quite believe he'd want her to stay after he'd witnessed her falling to pieces.

He smiled, relief pouring through him. 'Of course. Lead the way.'

Leaving the room hand in hand, they climbed the stairs and he guided her into his bedroom. Once in there they both lay down on the bed, facing each other but keeping a small distance between them. He wasn't sure what she needed from him, but he was prepared to wait until she was ready to tell him.

Her eyes looked tired and red from crying but she didn't break her gaze from his, clearly comfortable in the knowledge that he sincerely didn't give two hoots about what she looked like right then.

She took a deep breath. 'I'm sorry about yesterday,' she said, her brow furrowing. 'It was stupid of me to let my exec producer assume we were engaged. I was being selfish, only thinking about myself—as usual—and you got caught in the crossfire.'

He shook his head. 'Forget about it. It's not important.'

'But it *is*. It's what I do, Theo. I cause chaos wherever I go. It's not fair to keep mixing you up in that.'

'Let me decide whether it's fair or not, okay?' he said, quietly but firmly. The last thing he wanted was to add to her worries with something that could be dealt with another time.

She let out a small huff of laughter. 'Why are you still around? Most men I know would have run for the hills by now.'

'Well, to coin a phrase, I'm not most men. I'm me. And I want to be here with you because you're my friend and I care about you.'

She stared at him, her eyes wide with insecurity. 'You care about me?'

His heart seemed to stutter in his chest. 'Yes.'

He wanted to say more. To tell her the whole truth.

But he couldn't do it. He couldn't make himself form the words.

She closed her eyes but didn't say anything. When she opened them again they were full of pain. 'I don't know why.'

He put a hand up to her face and stroked his thumb down her cheek. 'Don't you? Really?'

CHAPTER NINE

EMILY STARED AT Theo's handsome face, which was dark with concern, and felt heady with confusion.

He cared about her?

And he'd stuck by her. Even when she'd pushed him away.

She hadn't wanted to break down in front of him and let him see her ugly, mangled innards splayed out in full view, but despite her best efforts to repel him he'd stood firm. Even more surprisingly he was *still* here, listening to her as if she was the most important person in the world to him right now.

What had she done to deserve this? She didn't know. She'd been nothing but manipulative and greedy around him recently, but he still hadn't pushed her away.

He was too good for her. He should be with someone kind and good and caring. Someone like Lula. Not a messed-up, selfish she-devil like her.

Reaching out a hand, she cupped his jaw and drew his head towards her, wanting to kiss the concern off his face and let him know how much she appreciated all that he'd done for her.

He kissed her back, gently and carefully, as if he was holding back a base urge to roll on top of her and slide their bodies together.

The thought of it made her insides flash with heat and a low, familiar throb began deep within her body, radiating out to make every nerve-ending zing with a yearning, aching need.

Pressing her mouth harder against his, she felt him give in to it and heard him groan low and deep in his throat.

Rolling on top of him, she pressed her body against his from chest to thigh, feeling the hard length of him against her hip. She rubbed against him, needing him to touch her, to make her feel good, to give her respite from the confusion of thoughts swirling round her head. But he kept his hands to himself, letting her do what she wanted to him, allowing her to use his body, to find comfort in the physical connection of it without asking for anything in return.

She needed this.

So much.

Oblivion.

Even if it was only for a short time.

Moving up to sit astride him, she unbuckled his belt with shaking fingers and pulled open his fly, releasing the hard length of him from the confines of his trousers.

Looking down at him, she saw he was staring at her intently, a muscle flicking in his jaw, and relief rushed through her as he gave a small nod of encouragement. Locating a condom in the bedside table, she rolled it onto him. Then, pulling her underwear to one side, she positioned herself over him and pushed down, feeling him fill and stretch her, hitting her deep inside her body.

It felt so right.

So good.

At that moment all she needed was to lose herself in

something wholesome, something comforting, something pure.

The tears came again as she moved, and she let them fall without attempting to stop them or brush them away. This was catharsis, expelling from her body all the hurt and anxiety she'd been bottling up since Theo had first confronted her last night.

His breathing was low and ragged as she rode him, his eyes screwed tightly shut as if he was concentrating hard on giving in to her. She loved him for that—for his total surrender to her whims and needs.

She moved faster and harder against him and she felt him grab the sheet beneath him, as if trying to hold back his release. The mere thought of him coming beneath her tipped her over the edge of her own control and she exploded with sensation, her breath rasping in her throat, and she called out to him, urging him to follow her.

He did as she asked, grasping her hips hard and rocking her back and forth on top of him, thrusting into her until he came too, letting out a low, guttural groan of relief.

Once their breathing had steadied she rolled off him and snuggled into his hot body. After he'd disposed of the condom he slid his arm beneath her neck so he could pull her against him more effectively.

They lay like that for a while, quiet and caught in their own thoughts.

'At least my mother finally got what she wanted,' she whispered eventually against his chest.

He put out a hand and stroked her cheek lightly, as if trying to smooth away her pain.

'I wasn't brave enough to forgive her, Theo, and now it's too late.' Her voice shook with the emotion she'd been keeping in check for so long. Too long.

'It's not your fault, Emily, you mustn't blame yourself.'

'Then who *is* to blame?'

'No one. No one could have predicted any of it. There were too many people involved, too many secrets.'

'Secrets,' she said. 'I knew they'd come back to bite me eventually.'

He snorted, pulling back to give her a wry smile.

'Are you ever going to tell me any of yours?' she asked tentatively.

The smile dropped from his lips and he shut his eyes, his brow pulling into a frown. 'Yeah, I guess I owe you an explanation about why I've been so distant with you.'

His voice held a twang of discomfort and she twisted away and up, so she could rest her head on the pillow next to him. From the tone of his voice she guessed it had to be something pretty serious.

He ran a hand over his face, apparently gearing himself up to tell his story.

'When my brother Hugo died I was in a tough place emotionally. I met a woman—Lauren—not long after it happened at the local pub. She seemed to appear out of the blue at the exact time I needed someone to talk to. Hugo's death had hit my parents hard, and I found it virtually impossible to talk to them about it. I guess what I'm trying to say is that I felt isolated, and suddenly there she was—all bright and fun and full of life, with all these wild ideas. A bit like you,' he said, shooting her a look that appealed for understanding. 'I fell for her hook, line and sinker,' he said, pulling his gaze away from hers and staring up at the ceiling.

He took a breath and blew it out slowly.

'I found out later that she'd latched on to me after seeing a piece in the newspaper about Hugo's death and how I was now first in line to be the Earl of Berkeley.

Apparently she fancied herself as Lady Berkeley. I'd had women trying to worm their way into my affections before, but she was something else.'

He shook his head in wonder.

'She had me totally fooled that she was for real. I guess because I was feeling so vulnerable about losing Hugo, and also because I was lonely—stuck out at the estate on my own after the sociability of university.'

'That's totally understandable, Theo, you shouldn't feel bad about that.'

He glanced over at her and gave her a sad smile. 'My parents hated her from the start. She wasn't the *"right sort of partner"* for me. Meaning she didn't come from a privileged and wealthy background. They called her behind my back and asked her to go over to the house and see them. When she got there they told her they'd cut off my inheritance if she continued to have a relationship with me. Then they offered to pay her off to leave me.'

'How underhand,' she said, feeling a sting of anger on his behalf.

'When she told me this, stupidly I told her that I'd give it all up for her and we should go off somewhere together and make a go of it without my family's money.' He glanced at her, his eyes hard. 'She was pregnant.'

'Oh, *no*, Theo!' Emily's stomach swooped and her skin grew hot and prickly as adrenaline woke her from her lazy stupor. She sat up, looking down at him as he lay on his back, staring at the ceiling.

'Apparently that wasn't *at all* what she wanted from the situation—or me—so she went behind my back and accepted my parents' pay-off, then aborted my child. I never saw or heard from her again after that.'

It took Emily a moment to fully process everything he'd told her. Her chest ached in sympathy for him. 'Are you positive she didn't keep the baby?' she asked eventually.

'Yes. She showed me the medical records from the hospital.'

'Oh, Theo, it's not surprising you don't trust women.'

'I spent a few years hating myself for being such a fool. I did some stuff that I'm not proud of. I used people. Hurt them. Including some of my friends. All to try and make myself feel better—less ashamed, less disgusted by how gullible I'd been. I was determined not to be taken in again, so I made sure no one ever got close enough to hurt me.'

He sighed and swiped a hand over his face.

'Obviously my parents heard about how I was living my life and tried to intervene again. They were afraid I was giving the Berkeley family a bad name. When I wouldn't listen my father cut off my trust fund, changed his will and told me if I didn't stop my philandering ways I'd never inherit the estate. I found myself with no money, no friends, and an uncertain future. It was the wake-up call I needed. I cleaned myself up, got a job at an engineering firm in London and gave up women. Then my father died suddenly, without changing his will, and everything went to my mother. While she was pleased I'd calmed down she wanted grandchildren, and when it became apparent I'd gone totally the other way and shut myself off from even *considering* a serious relationship, she started making veiled threats about keeping the house from me for good. And then not so veiled threats.'

'No wonder she's been so picky about who you get involved with,' Emily said carefully.

'Well, I am too. I'm *very* careful now. I don't have meaningless sex and I *always* check someone out thoroughly before I commit to having any kind of relationship with them. I'm a very private person and I hate the idea of everyone knowing my business. That's why I was so hard on you about the press invasion into my life.'

She flopped back onto the pillow next to him, a deep sense of shame mixing with the heady feeling of finally understanding where he was coming from. No wonder he'd hated her antics in dragging him into the media spotlight. She'd put him through his worst nightmare. *Twice.*

'Theo, I'm so sorry about what happened with the press—' she began, but he put up a hand to halt her.

'You've already apologised, Emily. It's over now. We don't need to talk about it again.'

Swallowing hard, she nodded against the pillow but didn't say anything, experiencing a horrifying sense of grief. Because there really couldn't be any kind of future for them now. She needed to be in the limelight for her career—and to make her happy—but he clearly abhorred the idea of it.

How did you get past something like that?

She'd been an idiot, thinking his confession about how he cared for her and the subsequent insight into his past meant there might be a chance for them when in fact it confirmed the opposite. They could never make a real relationship work. They needed totally different things.

He rolled over and slung an arm across her shoulders, dragging her against his chest. She let him hold her there, sinking into the heat and strength of his body, this time holding back the hot tears that threatened to spill from her eyes.

After a minute or two she heard his breathing level out and felt him relax into sleep, his arm still draped across her possessively.

It felt like the beginning of the end.

* * *

Emily woke the next morning to find herself alone in bed.

After getting dressed, she traipsed downstairs wearily, her entire body feeling heavy and stiff from all the tension she'd been holding on to.

It was important to her not to show Theo how exposed she was feeling about what had happened last night. She needed to be able to walk away with her head held high so she had to keep things light from this point onwards.

She felt sure that right about now he must be wondering how to get her out of his house without seeming callous anyway. She'd put a lot of pressure on him in the last couple of days, dealing with her grief, and their already fragile relationship—or whatever the hell it was—was already under immense strain. The last thing she wanted was to outstay her welcome, so she decided she'd go back to London after they'd had breakfast.

To give them both a breather from the intensity of being together under such difficult circumstances.

To start the process of giving him up.

She found him in the kitchen, making his regulation strong coffee, and placed an empty mug down next to his, giving him a supplicatory smile.

'Need. Coffee,' she joked, going for levity.

He gave her a grim smile and poured some of the dark, fragrant liquid from the jug into her mug.

'You're a very kind man,' she said, blowing him a kiss and taking her drink over to the table, where his housekeeper had left a range of the day's newspapers out for him.

She flicked the top one to the front page and ran her gaze over it while he walked over to join her at the table.

It took her a moment to realise what she was actually seeing.

When it finally sank in, her whole body froze in shock, causing him first to glance over at her with a frown, then down at what she was reading.

It wasn't good.

Oh, no.

It really wasn't.

There was a picture of the two of them at her mother's funeral, with her gripping Theo's hand possessively as the coffin was lowered into the ground. There appeared to be a dispassionate, almost haughty look on her face as Theo frowned at her.

Above it ran the unsubtle headline: *Treasure Trail's Emily Applegate begs her earl fiancé to take her away from all this madness.*

It went on to detail all the facts about her mother's illness and secret hospitalisation, and how the affliction might be hereditary, going on further to speculate about her own private life and ask whether her 'wild ways' had anything to do with the possibility that she might be 'on the wrong side of crazy' herself.

It would have been truly entertaining reading if it hadn't been *her* life they'd ripped apart in under five hundred words.

'It must have been that blasted journalist from the film premiere,' Theo muttered, swiping a hand through his hair. 'She walked into the corridor just after we'd had that shouting match. Perhaps she heard more than we realised?'

'It's entirely likely.' Her whole body felt heavy with misery.

'She must have followed us from your house to the funeral. In fact, thinking about it now, I distinctly remember seeing what I thought was the reflection of the sun on a camera lens.'

Emily sighed and dropped into the chair next to him. 'Well, there you go. The mystery of how the most painful day of my life came to be splashed over the papers for all the world to laugh and gossip about solved.'

It was all her fault, of course. She'd brought it on herself by craving the limelight. In fact she'd actively sought it out.

She looked at Theo, standing there with that fierce look she'd grown to know and love on his face, and felt something die inside her.

It had been fun while it lasted, her and Theo—more fun than she'd had in a long while…maybe ever—but it was over now. It had to be.

'Well, I guess we're screwed.'

He frowned. 'What do you mean, *we*?'

'Your mother's going to *love* it when she reads about what a great choice you've made for a wife.' She laid on so much sarcasm she saw him blanch.

'She might not see it,' he said, sounding totally unconvinced.

She gave a sarcastic laugh. 'She'll see it. The *Daily Courier*'s one of the most syndicated newspapers in the world and the story will be all over the internet. People love it when a celebrity crashes and burns—it's like having a big juicy bone to pick over. And I suspect your mother's friends will be keen to point it out to her as soon as they see it too.'

She got up wearily from the table and walked out of the kitchen without another word.

He didn't try and stop her, and she didn't blame him. What was the point?

She was stuffing yesterday's outfit into her weekend bag, trying to ignore the way her hands were shaking, when he walked into the bedroom and stopped dead, staring at her in confusion.

'What are you doing?'

'What does it look like I'm doing? I'm leaving.'

'Why?'

She frowned and shook her head, feigning incredulity. 'We can't have any kind of contact now. Your mum's going to find out about me and my crazy family and want me away from you pronto—I can guarantee it.'

He moved towards her and put his hand on her bag, stopping her from zipping it up. 'What if I don't want you to go?'

She shot him a grimace. 'Then you lose everything—your home, your business, your pride.' She shook her head and pushed his hand away from the zip so she could do it up. 'You don't want to be mixed up with someone like me, Theo. I do bad things—like lying about my mother being dead and persuading you to walk straight into a press ambush by using sex as a weapon.'

'You don't care that we'll never see each other again?' His voice sounded gruff and unsteady.

A hot torrent of guilt flooded through her, leaving a stinging resentment in its wake.

'Hell, Theo, what do you want me to say? That I'm madly in love with you and want to turn this farce into a real relationship? That I want you to give everything up for me? That I want hearts and flowers now?'

'Do you?'

She turned to face him and her breath caught painfully in her throat at the look of hope on his face. 'No, Theo, I don't. And you don't really want me. I'm selfish and self-absorbed and quite possibly *"on the wrong side of crazy"*.'

He snorted angrily. 'Is that what you're worried about?

That you'll suffer with depression like your mother and I'll shove you away into some institution? You know you shouldn't believe everything you read in the papers,' he said, evidently trying to keep his tone light, but still managing to sound like his usual ferocious self.

She shook her head. 'No. I know you'd never do that to me.'

'Then stay. Give us a chance,' he said quietly.

She swallowed hard. 'I can't, Theo.'

Throwing his hands up in frustration, he paced away from her, then strode back, cupping her face in his hands, his gaze intense with determination. 'Please, Emily.'

She stared at him in shock for one regret-filled moment, before closing herself down and shaking her head, loosening his grip on her.

'You're crazy if you think it's a good idea to risk your inheritance for me. You'll regret it and blame me, and I'm not prepared to be your emotional punchbag. That's not how I play.'

This time he put a hand on each arm and dragged her close, but she looked away, avoiding his gaze.

'You're scared and upset. I understand why, but you can't let fear take over your whole life. You need to face it some time. I'll always be here for you, Emily.' He waited until she looked him in the eye again. 'I've got your back.'

She had to fight to hold back the angry, frustrated tears. She couldn't do it to him. She'd never be able to live with herself if she let him down again—which, based on past experience, she was bound to do. It would break her heart if she sent him back into the black funk of his years after the Lauren incident. She couldn't be responsible for causing him more pain than he'd already gone through—especially after he'd worked so hard to pull himself out of the darkness and do something good with his life. He helped people. Really made a difference to their lives. A positive one. Unlike her.

She loved him too much to drag him down with her.

She loved him?

She loved him.

Oh, heaven help her, she loved him.

Her whole chest felt so tight with fear and confusion and rage at the unfairness of it all she thought she might burst.

She had to get out of there. Right now. Before she did something stupid like telling him how she really felt about him.

Looking him dead in the eye, she said, 'I'm not going to change my mind, Theo. Let me go.'

He stared at her. 'So that's it? You're just going to leave?'

Her nod was curt and definite. 'Yes.'

'And that's your final word?'

His eyes were wide and haunted, and she knew if she didn't get away from him right now she'd lose the courage to walk away.

'No, this is.' She leant forward and brushed her lips gently against his.

Before he could put his arms around her to stop her she backed away.

'Goodbye.'

Back in London, she let herself into her house on autopilot and took a shower, washing the smell of Theo off her for the last time, holding back the tears that pressed painfully against the back of her eyes.

When she got out she drank a long slug of wine straight from the bottle.

It didn't help one bit.

Pacing around didn't help either.

Her eyes felt hot and aching with unshed tears, but she was determined not to give in to it.

She wouldn't cry. She *wouldn't.*

'Shake it off, Emily, shake it off,' she muttered to herself, flapping her hands about and letting out a maniacal laugh when she thought about how crazy she'd seem to anyone looking in.

That numb, floaty feeling that she'd had after hearing her mother had died was back—only this time it was joined by a low pull of horror, deep in her belly.

She was never going to be able to see Theo again.

And it was all her own fault.

She'd been so busy trying to plug the gaps in her life with the meaningless adoration of strangers that she'd put herself in a position where nobody *real* could get near her without getting hurt.

Her mobile rang and she grabbed it quickly, glad of the distraction. Her heart-rate spiked as saw the name of the executive producer of *Treasure Trail* flash onto the screen.

'Ben, tell me something good. Please. I'm begging you.'

There was a small pause. 'I'm sorry, Emily, it's bad news.'

She slumped down onto the sofa. Of course it was. How could it be anything else?

'After a lot of discussion we've decided to go with Daisy Dunlop as the new face of *Treasure Trail*,' he went on. 'The station was pushing heavily for someone of her stature to take over, and unfortunately the story about you in the papers today was a deal-breaker for them. They felt your image wasn't quite in line with theirs.'

'Right.'

'I swear, Emily, I fought for you all the way.'

'Of course you did, Ben.' She was too exhausted by it all even to inject enough venom into the sentence to give it the cynical twist it needed.

'Look, I'm sorry. I'm sure you'll pick up something else great soon. You've a real talent, and that's not going to be overlooked for long.'

'Thanks,' she said dully, desperate to end the call now.

'Okay. Well, I'm sorry again, and I want to wish you the very best of luck for the future.'

The future. Her bright, shiny future.

It had all turned to dust.

CHAPTER TEN

THEO DIDN'T GET out of bed for two days.

He hoped she'd call or just turn up on his doorstep in her usual carefree manner—even if it was only to return an article of clothing she'd borrowed from him—just so he could see her again.

God, he missed her.

But he knew she wasn't coming back. She didn't love him—not enough to fight for him anyway. She'd made that clear.

He actually ached inside from the misery of it.

Finally, on the third day, he pulled himself together and got up and took a shower, barely feeling the stinging hot water on his numbed skin.

He'd just got himself dressed and padded downstairs to make himself an extra-strong cup of coffee when there was a loud knock at the door.

His heart leapt into his throat, making the pounding in his head from two days' worth of caffeine deprivation double in intensity, as he pictured Emily's beautiful remorseful face in his mind.

Racing to the door, he yanked it open—only to have his stomach sink to the floor at the sight of his mother standing on the doorstep.

She frowned at him, apparently surprised by his appearance. 'Theo? Are you all right?'

The very last thing he wanted was to have to explain himself to his mother.

'Are you and Emily engaged?' his mother asked, her brow arched and the look in her eyes intent.

He folded his arms across his chest. 'No.'

She frowned and her face seemed to fall a little.

Odd.

'Then why did it say that in the newspaper?' she asked tersely.

'Because there was a miscommunication.'

'A what?'

'They misreported something, Mother.'

'Right.' She nodded once, then gave him an expectant look. 'Well, aren't you going to let me in?'

He sighed. But he couldn't very well turn her away from her own house.

'Yes. Come in. I was about to make some coffee. Would you like some?'

'I'll take a tea, darling. I don't touch coffee. It gives me a headache, remember?'

'Yes, of course.'

She was giving *him* a headache.

In the kitchen she accepted her drink with a grateful nod and took a sip before turning her attention on him again.

'So where is Emily now?'

'London, I guess. I don't know. We're not involved any more.'

He was surprised to see his mother's face drop again. 'Why ever not?'

'You saw the article, Mother. She didn't think you'd be too keen on having her join the family.'

She shook her head as if trying to clear it. 'I don't understand.'

He lost patience with her. 'Look, I know you don't think she's good enough to further the Berkeley family line, or some such rubbish, but I don't want anyone else. Sell the house, if that's what you want. I don't care any more. There are one too many bad memories here now anyway.'

Her expression was confused. 'I'm not going to sell the house, Theo, it belongs to you.'

'No, it doesn't.'

'Not yet—legally, at least—but I've decided to sign it over to you. This silly feud between us has gone on too long.'

He stared at her, trying to process what she'd just said. 'You're selling me the house?'

'I'm *giving* it to you.'

He let out an involuntary huff of surprise. 'Why?'

'Because it belongs to you and you belong to it. I never much enjoyed living here—I prefer more modern buildings—but I know that you love it here.'

He shook his head wearily. 'It won't make a difference to anything. Emily doesn't want me.'

'Are you sure?'

He slammed his coffee mug down on the table, feeling the burning liquid slop over his hand but not caring. 'You can't fix this, Mother, so don't even bother trying. This is one problem you can't *buy* your way out of.'

Getting up, he marched out of the house and over to the workshop, turning on all the machines and finding a strange kind of peace in the grinding and whirring noise of their engines.

He was so *angry*.

He'd been punishing himself all these years for things he'd not been able to predict or control—and for what?

To be alone and miserable still.

He'd held everyone at a safe distance from him until Emily had shaken it out of him—but look what had happened.

Once again he'd found himself willing to give up everything—something he'd sworn never to do again—but it hadn't been enough.

He'd still lost the best thing that had ever happened to him.

Sighing, he slumped down against the wall, putting his head in his hands.

It was over. She wasn't coming back.

He just needed to find a way to live without her now.

Emily was busily scrubbing the doors of her dining room, just for something to take her mind off the incessant loop of sadness and anger and loneliness swirling through her head, when there was a ring on her doorbell.

Dumping the cloth in the bucket of water, she went to the door, fully expecting to have to turn away a determined salesperson—only to find Theo's mother standing there, looking completely incongruous, somehow, the epitome of a fish out of water. The woman was far too genteel to be standing in the middle of a busy London street.

'Francesca! How did you find me?' Surely the woman hadn't tracked her down here just to tell her to leave her son alone?

Francesca gave a small cough behind her hand before speaking. 'Theo's housekeeper found your address out for me—she didn't need much persuasion to help. Apparently she really likes you and thinks you're a good match for Theo.'

She patted down her immaculate hair and raised an eyebrow.

'She told him that you'd lent her something and she wanted to post it back.' Her expression levelled out until she looked almost contrite. 'I couldn't ask him directly. I think he might have thrown me out of a window if I had.'

She gave a terse smile. The woman clearly found it difficult to tell a joke. What a curse *that* must be.

'What can I do for you, Francesca?' Emily asked, pulling herself together now she'd got over the shock of seeing Theo's mother on her doorstep.

'I wonder whether I could come in and talk to you? I have a few things I need to tell you.'

She frowned. 'About Theo?'

'Yes. And about me.'

Nodding slowly, wondering what the hell she was about to be told and accepting that she didn't have the strength to refuse to hear it, she backed up so the woman could walk into her hallway. She realised that any link with Theo at this point was better than the nothing she'd been living with since she'd walked away from him.

'Come into the living room,' she said, leading the way.

Francesca walked over to one of her sofas and positioned herself daintily on the edge of it, waiting for her to sit down opposite before she began speaking.

'I heard that your mother passed away. I wanted to offer my greatest sympathies,' she said, her eyes soft and kind.

'Thank you, Francesca.' Emily was taken aback by the woman's opening gambit. She'd expected nothing less than a severe dressing-down.

'So your mother didn't go to school in France, then?' Francesca asked, with a meaningful look in her eye.

Ah, so here it came…

'No.'

'She went to a boarding-school here, didn't she? *My* old school?'

'Yes.'

'I thought so.'

She moved back on the sofa a little and crossed her legs, as if settling in for a comfy chat.

'I knew your mother at school. Not well, but I always liked her. She was really kind to me once. I was being bullied and she chased them off. They never bothered me again. Even back then it was clear she suffered from malaise at times, though.'

She shook her head and smiled sadly.

Emily felt a strange weight lifting from her, as if Francesca's version of her mother somehow rounded out all the other memories she had of her. The ones of when they had laughed and played and had fun together. Before she'd got sad and had flown into unpredictable violent rages, and taken to her bed a lot.

'I knew I recognised you from somewhere,' Francesca continued, apparently unaware of the intensity of the sorrow she'd caused to flood through Emily's whole body. 'You're very much like your mother. You have the same mannerisms. The same hair and eyes.'

'Yeah, I heard that a lot when I was young. Before she…' Emily paused, realising she no longer had to reel out the lie that had almost become the truth in her mind over the years. 'Before she was committed.'

Francesca nodded, seemingly accepting the confession without any kind of difficulty. 'Theo is very much like *me* in many ways,' she said, raising her eyebrows and pursing her lips. 'It's not surprising we butt heads all the time.'

Emily smiled sadly at her, trying not to dwell on how she butted heads with Theo too because it only made the sorrow intensify.

'I suppose that's why we never got on too well when he was younger. I'm guessing he told you about the woman he got mixed up with right after Hugo's death? And the wild behaviour he indulged in afterwards?'

Her gaze locked with Emily's and Emily saw regret there.

'Yes. He did tell me a bit about that.'

'The thing you have to know, Emily, is that I knew what that Lauren woman was doing the first time I met her, and I so desperately wanted to save him from the pain of what was about to happen. Unfortunately, in my grief at losing Hugo, I didn't handle things too well.'

'No. That's what Theo told me,' she said, knowing there was no point in trying to placate the woman.

Francesca huffed out a sigh and looked down at her perfectly manicured fingernails. 'She latched on to Theo after Hugo's funeral. I could see her for what she was right away: a gold-digger. I was suspicious about how quickly she appeared after Hugo's death and fell for him. I love my son dearly, but as I'm sure you've noticed he can be a little hard to get to know. He was always like that—reserved. He had good friends, and he got on famously with his brother, but he was usually wary of people he didn't know because of his family background. So I hired a private detective to check up on her and he came back with some worrying information. A previous very short marriage and debt. Lots of debt. I did what any good mother would do for her son. I tested her with the threat of taking away his money and she failed. He had a narrow escape.'

Emily was shocked by the extent of the trouble the woman had gone to. But then maybe that was par for the course when you were part of a titled family with a large estate and bank balance.

'Does Theo know about what the private detective found out?'

Francesca sighed. 'I tried to tell him at the time but he blanked me. I think he didn't want to believe it was true. He was in love with her. Or he thought he was.'

'Yeah, it's very easy to be taken in by people when you're young and trusting,' Emily muttered.

Francesca clasped her hands together, as if asking for forgiveness for what she was about to say.

'I feel dreadful about what happened with Lauren, but I'm not sorry she left him. Clearly she was manipulative. After we warned her off she came back to Theo's father and me and asked for a pay-off. Said she'd leave Theo alone if we gave her money.'

Emily frowned. 'She came to *you*? Theo thinks you offered *her* money.'

'No. That's not how it happened.' Francesca sighed and shook her head. 'Poor Theo. His pride was understandably damaged, of course, but it was for the best. Not that he ever saw it that way. He's been torturing me all these years—first of all with the wild behaviour he indulged in for a time after it happened, then with his determination not to get seriously involved with anyone again.'

Francesca looked at Emily with such a wretched expression it made her chest constrict in sympathy.

'I didn't just lose one son, Emily, I lost two,' she said, her voice now choked with emotion.

Emily instinctively reached out and put her hand on Francesca's. 'That must have been hard for you.'

'It was. Truly awful. He blamed me, of course, for Lauren leaving, and he still hasn't forgiven me.'

'Perhaps that's because of the baby,' she said, giving the woman a mindful frown.

Francesca's eyes widened in shock. 'What baby?' she gasped.

Emily's jaw dropped in surprise. 'You didn't know? Lauren was pregnant and she had an abortion once you'd paid her off.'

'I didn't know. Theo never told me. Oh, goodness.' Francesca buried her head in her hands and stared at the floor in shock. 'My poor Theo. I never would have—what did I *do?*'

Emily leant forward and rubbed her shoulder, really feeling for the woman now. There had been more than one victim in the Berkeley family too.

If only they'd all talked to each other more.

'It's not your fault, Francesca. How could you have known if they didn't tell you?'

'No wonder he wouldn't speak to me for so long after it happened. It took until after his father's death, a few years ago, before he'd give me more than a few cursory words of information about what he was doing. I suppose I always expected great things from him and put him under a lot of pressure to conform to that. The whole nobility thing can be both a blessing and a curse. I thought maybe that was why he avoided me for so long.'

She sighed and swiped away a tear from under her eye.

'I probably shouldn't have agreed to let him live in the manor house after I moved out. It only seemed to make him more reclusive. That's why I made all those ridiculous threats about selling the place—to try and make things right. I thought a threat of losing the house was the way to shake him up a little and pull him out of that stubborn funk. To get him to fight for something that meant something to him. I guess it worked after all, because that something turned out to be you.'

She turned her gaze on Emily and gave her a hopeful smile.

'Look, Francesca—'

'I'm giving him the house, Emily. Now he has you to share it with.'

She stared at the woman in shock, her head spinning with the sudden turn in conversation. 'It wouldn't work out with us, Francesca. I'm not a good person. I'm selfish and irresponsible.'

'Rubbish! You're a wonderful person and you're going to make my son very happy. And he'll make you happy too, if you let him.' She put a reassuring hand on Emily's arm. 'Don't be afraid. He'll love and protect you ferociously.'

Francesca's approval made Emily heady with exhilaration as she realised she was finally being accepted into a family with genuine warmth and love. In fact, if she allowed herself to trust that Theo could really, truly love her—and judging by the way he'd taken care of her recently she felt deep down that he could, if she let him—then she'd be gaining a mother at the same time as reconciling with the love of her life.

Francesca clearly felt she hadn't quite won her over yet, though, because she smiled and tipped her head in contrition. 'Look, I'm sorry I was so unfriendly when we first met. I suspected you might just be a friend of his—putting on a show for my benefit so that I'd leave him alone. But when I saw the two of you together I knew that couldn't be right. There's this powerful intensity between you that I've never witnessed in him before. Whenever you're in the same room he can't keep his eyes off you.'

Emily knew it was time to fess up. It would be cruel and wrong to keep Francesca in the dark about their manipulative little plan any longer. Especially after she'd just been so honest with *her*.

'It *was* a show, Francesca. I'd only met Theo the day before you met me. I wanted my best friend to be allowed to have her wedding at your house and at that point I was prepared to do anything to make it happen.'

Francesca laughed quietly. 'Well, you could have fooled me—in fact, you did. I never would have guessed you weren't both totally infatuated with each other. The air seemed to hum around you.'

'That would have been our *exasperation* with each other.'

Francesca shook her head. 'No. It was definitely something else. Something powerful. And there's no exasperation now, am I right?'

'Well, I don't know about that. He can be really pig-headed when he wants to be. As can I.'

'That's why you're so good for him. It takes a special woman to handle someone as complex as Theo. Before he met you it was as if he was deliberately choosing women who wouldn't challenge him. They were never going to last long.' She sighed. 'Lauren well and truly damaged his confidence.'

Emily stared at the floor, her heart racing. 'I'm afraid I might damage him even more, though, Francesca. I'm not an easy person to live with. I'm wild and impetuous and frustrating and self-centred.'

'He loves you, Emily. He loves all those things about you. I can see it in him. He's not allowed anyone else to get close to him again after what happened with Lauren, but you've brought him out of his shell. Please don't give up on him.'

Emily looked up into the other woman's eyes. 'I thought you wouldn't want me involved in your family after you found out about my mother. And her illness.'

Francesca's expression was one of horror. 'Of course not! What do you take me for?'

Emily shrugged, feeling the stiffness in her tense shoulders. 'I don't know. I've had to live with this thing hanging over me for so long I think I've lost all perspective on it.'

'Well, that's understandable, but you can't let it run your life any more—you're stronger than that, Emily. I know you are.'

'Maybe.'

'And you love Theo?' Francesca asked gently.

Emily thought about how she felt when she was with him. How comforted and excited and inspired. How he'd taken care of her when she'd needed him the most, even though he was furious with her for using him to try and keep her job. And she'd been cruel to him. A cruelty that he'd never deserved. Then she thought about how miserable she'd be if she never got to hold and kiss him or laugh with him again.

'Yes. I love him,' she said, not even bothering to battle back the tears that finally welled in her eyes and began to spill down her cheeks.

'Then go and tell him,' Francesca said firmly.

She nodded and smiled, her whole body hot with a mixture of excitement and nerves.

'Yes. I think I will.'

Theo was in his workshop again.

In fact he'd hardly left it since his mother had appeared

to let him know the house was now his to do with what he wanted. He could even go back to holding wedding receptions here now without fear of reprisals, if he chose to, but the thought of it only depressed him.

Everything seemed flat and grey since Emily had walked away from him—as if she'd taken the light and colour with her—and he was having trouble summoning the energy to do anything but lose himself in his work.

He was just finishing off some welding on a new device he'd invented, to help a woman who'd lost an arm in a car accident to carry heavy things around the house, when he noticed in his peripheral vision that someone was standing in the doorway to the workshop.

He blinked hard, still seeing stars from the welding, until his vision cleared and he realised that the figure belonged to someone familiar. Someone so familiar it made his heart thump hard in his chest.

Emily.

He stared at her, wondering whether he was actually hallucinating. 'You came back,' he finally managed to get past the sudden tension in his throat.

'I did. It seems I couldn't stay away,' she said, moving into the room towards him.

'Why are you here?'

'For you. I came back for you.'

He just kept staring at her, barely able to believe what he was hearing. He'd thought he'd lost her for good—that the newspaper article and his mother's supposed wrath had been just a good excuse for her to leave without giving him a way back to her. To keep him at arm's length for ever.

'I need to warn you, though: I'm not going to be easy to live with. I need a lot of attention. A *lot*.'

He couldn't help but let out a huff of pained laughter. 'Yes, I noticed that.'

She nodded slowly and made her way over to him, stopping a foot away, still keeping a small distance between them.

'I just wanted to be adored, Theo, for so many years, and I thought being in the public eye would fill that need. But it never did. Not the way I wanted it to anyway. It made me more egoistic, more self-centred, and I found myself doing more and more outrageous things to get attention. After a while I lost all sense of what was and wasn't reasonable behaviour. I'm talking about using people and casting them off before they could get too close. Not the sex, though. I'll never apologise for enjoying sex,' she said, flipping him a tentative grin.

He smiled and rolled his eyes in jest.

'Anyway,' she said, shrugging a shoulder. 'It seems that all that narcissistic behaviour well and truly came back to haunt me, and I was terrified about it affecting you too, knowing you as I do now.'

He frowned and shook his head. 'You know, you're the best thing that ever happened to me. You forced me to stop hiding and experience life again. I wouldn't be half the person I am now if I hadn't met you, Emily. I finally started *living* again.'

She dropped her gaze. 'I want to deserve you, Theo. I want to be the woman to make you happy. I'm just afraid I'll fail and hurt you, and that's the last thing I want to do.' Looking up, she locked her gaze with his again, her expression open and sincere and her bottom lip trembling slightly. 'Because I love you. I'm *in* love with you.'

Stepping forward to close the gap between them, he cupped her face in his hands, drawing her forward and kissing her hard, attempting to relay his utter joy at hearing those words as relief poured through him.

It seemed he might have succeeded, because when he drew away from her again her eyes were bright with tears and happiness.

'I'm willing to risk anything if it means I get to have you, Emily. Because I love you too,' he said, looking deep into her incredible golden eyes and feeling the connection with her deep in his soul.

'We're a proper pair, the two of us,' she said, her voice thick with emotion.

'That's exactly what we are—a pair. Two halves of a whole.'

She grinned and raised both eyebrows. 'There's a dirty joke in there somewhere.'

'Let's leave it for another time,' he said with a good-humoured frown, pulling her in for another kiss.

There would be plenty of time for jokes later.

EPILOGUE

One year later

THEIR WEDDING VENUE was perfect.

It wasn't flashy or cool or grand—it was select and tasteful and comfortable.

At least comfortable enough for the small gathering of friends and family who had come to see Theo and Emily get married.

After some discussion they'd agreed to keep it simple and had invited only Lula—who was her bridesmaid—and Tristan, of course, Theo's mother, Emily's brother, and a good friend of Theo's whom he'd known since university and who had gamely agreed to be best man.

It was just right for them; exactly what they'd both wanted in the end.

No press. No fuss. Just the people they loved.

It had been tough, keeping the secret of their engagement and then their impending nuptials from the press—especially as Emily had to remember to take off her engagement ring whenever she was filming in case anyone caught on.

The show she was now hosting and also executive producing had steadily and resoundingly beaten the ratings of *Treasure Trail with Daisy Dunlop* since the day it had launched.

Not that she was gloating about that fact.

Much.

More importantly, because of the power she wielded on the show as executive producer, Emily knew she'd never have to go through the stress of waiting to see whether she was going to be usurped by someone younger and more hungry for success than she was.

Not that she courted the press at all these days. All that craziness was well and truly behind her now.

She had a steady, comfortable life with Theo at the manor and she was happy.

More happy and settled than she'd ever been in her entire life.

'Well, you two, you did it,' Lula said to them, beaming with delight once they'd exchanged rings and kissed each other with the blessing of the registrar.

It was just like Lula to be ecstatic at the thought of another happy-ever-after; she was a starry-eyed dreamer, after all, who'd managed to make her own dreams come true.

'So, not meaning to grab the limelight on your big day, but…' She paused for effect, looping her arm through Tristan's and smiling around at them all with big, mischievous eyes.

Emily's heart began to race with anticipation and she had to dig her nails into her palms in an attempt not to shake the information out of her friend.

She really hated being kept in suspense.

'I'm pregnant,' Lula announced finally, her expression radiating the joy she clearly felt at this life-changing event.

'Whose is it?' Theo asked wryly, and was rewarded with a thump on the arm from both Lula and Emily.

He grinned nonchalantly at Lula and Tristan. 'But seriously, that's fantastic news, guys. Congratulations.'

After Emily had dragged her friend to her for a hug, and smothered her in kisses, Lula jumped up and down on the spot excitedly and blurted, 'So you two have to get a move on and get pregnant too, so we can have babies together!'

Tristan grinned at his wife and put a gentle restraining hand on her arm. 'Give them a chance, Lu, they've only just tied the knot.'

Lula's face flushed bright red and they all patted her back in support as she spluttered an apology.

'Don't worry, Lula, I'm sure it'll be on the cards soon enough,' Theo said, grinning at his wife.

Emily raised an eyebrow. 'Will it?'

'Yes, of course. We need to seriously think about extending the family line now we've validated the nuptials,' he said, stony-faced, and only broke into a smile when she jumped on him, grabbing him playfully around the neck and wrapping her legs around his waist—just able to manage it in her tightly fitting wedding dress.

'I think that's our cue to leave, Lu,' Tristan said, giving a bemused shake of his head. 'We'll see you back at your house.'

'Yeah, great,' Theo said. 'There should be champagne when you arrive—make sure you get some. Although…' he looked at Lula '…I guess you're not allowed any at the moment.'

She pouted, then grinned. 'I can live with that,' she said breezily, taking Tristan's hand and walking away with him.

'Are you going to get off me now?' Theo asked, his

voice sounding rather strained from holding Emily's weight against him.

She slid down his body, then readjusted the silky skirt of her dress. 'I'm off.'

'Glad to hear it.'

'Theo?' she breathed into his ear, leaning her body seductively against his.

'Wife?'

'About that baby…?'

He turned to give her a confused frown. 'I thought we'd agreed to wait a year and give ourselves some time to enjoy being married first?'

'Oh, yeah, I'm still on for that. It's just I was thinking…'

'Yeeess?'

'There's no harm in getting some *practice* in now, for when we're ready to start trying. Right?' she said, waggling her eyebrows at him and drawing him towards one of the quiet, lockable ante-rooms at the wedding venue.

'No harm at all,' he said with a grin. 'Lead on, Lady Berkeley.'

* * * * *

MILLS & BOON®

Spend your Christmas at the Snow Crystal resort

Sarah Morgan's latest trilogy is filled with memorable characters, wit, charm and heart-melting romance! Get your hands on all three stories this Christmas!

Visit
www.millsandboon.co.uk/snowcrystal

1214_ST_7